T0114887

Alister Jensen
THE CASE OF THE ENGRAVED RING

DONALD CHRISTOPHERSON

authorHOUSE®

AuthorHouse™
1663 Liberty Drive
Bloomington, IN 47403
www.authorhouse.com
Phone: 833-262-8899

Published by AuthorHouse 10/19/2020

ISBN: 978-1-6655-0443-0 (sc)
ISBN: 978-1-6655-0471-3 (e)

Library of Congress Control Number: 2020920469

Print information available on the last page.

Chapter 1

Alister looked up from his computer and noticed the lieutenant leave his office and walk across the squad room floor in his direction.

When the lieutenant arrived at Alister's cubicle he said, "A robbery-assault call just came in. Since you and your partner have a comparatively light caseload this month, you get the call."

He handed the call ticket to Alister and returned to his office. Alister Jensen and his partner, Richard Hopkins, had their desks up against opposite walls in their cubicle, so they sat back-to-back.

Richard swiveled his chair around and asked, "What did we get?"

"The ticket says that a Mr. Dubois was attacked in his apartment this morning and robbed. He returned home from the health clinic at 7:00 AM and telephoned the police," answered Alister.

"Where does he live?" asked Richard.

"1204 Third Avenue, Apartment 205," answered Alister. "Let's go."

They got their Glock 9 mm's from their desk drawers, coats from the coat tree, and left the cubicle. There were about 40 cubicles in the detective squad room. As they went down the center aisle, they noticed that half of the cubicles were empty. There were stacks of papers and photos on the desks along with open computers. The detectives were either out on calls or in the cafeteria.

As they entered the hall, Alister said, "Let's take the stairs. Waiting for the elevator in this five-story building tries my patience."

"Okay."

When they entered the garage in the basement they walked to their car. They had been issued a grey Ford with no police markings except for the number 74 on the rear trunk.

Richard got in the driver side and Alister took the passenger seat. Richard headed for the exit onto Columbia Street. As they drove up the ramp onto Columbia, Richard said, "Well it's raining again, but not very heavy."

They turned left and headed down the hill towards Third Avenue. They could see the Vashon Island ferry out in the Sound.

Alister said, "The sight of the ferry on its route always makes a tranquil scene. It just proceeds slowly and steadily on its journey."

"Yes, it's nice. It always favorably impresses all of our relatives when they come to visit Melanie and me," responded Richard.

When they arrived at 1204 Third Avenue, they noticed a marked squad car parked directly in front of the apartment building. This was a low income region of the city. Richard parked directly behind the squad car, and they went into the building.

A hallway led from the door to a staircase in the rear. To the left of the hallway was a living room or sitting room. Quite a few middle aged and old men were sitting there. They looked up and watched the police enter their domicile.

Alister and Richard made their way up the stairs to room 205 on the second floor. They knocked on the door and entered.

The patrol officers who took the 911 call were in the room questioning Mr. Dubois. Sergeant Johnson, who had his nameplate on his jacket, recognized Alister and said, "Good morning Alister. We took the 911 call and came to this address."

"Hello," answered Alister. "What do we have here?"

Sergeant Johnson leafed through his notebook and summarized their findings.

"We arrived at 7:10 AM and knocked on the door of room 205. Mr. DuBois, here, is the registered tenant. He informed us that he was awakened last night about 1:00 AM by an intruder in his room. He got into a scuffle with the intruder and was eventually knocked down. He observed the intruder put several items into a pillowcase and escape through that window," pointing at one of the two windows in the room.

Sergeant Johnson continued, "He considered calling the police and 911 right away. But he noticed he was bleeding some from a cut on his jaw and felt a bit banged up on his back. So, Mr. Dubois decided to go to the 24 hour clinic on Fourth and Pine Street first to get bandaged up before calling the police."

The sergeant closed his notebook and said, "Then Denise and I started questioning him about his missing property.

But we decided to wait until you people arrived from the detective bureau."

"All right sergeant, we can take it from here," said Alister.

The two uniformed officers left.

Alister looked at Mr. Dubois and asked, "How do you feel Mr. Dubois? Do you think you can answer some questions now?"

Mr. Dubois put his hand on his bandaged jaw and then moved it to his back. He winced a bit as he moved his shoulders but said, "Yeah, I can talk now. I suppose the sooner you get started on the culprit's trail, the more likely you will catch him."

Caspar DuBois looked to be about 45 years old. He was about 5 foot 8 inches in height and maybe 160 pounds in weight. He had brown hair and no beard or mustache. He had a nice smile and a friendly extroverted manner. He was wearing a gray sport coat and light blue shirt with no tie. He wore dark blue pants and black loafers.

"Mr. Dubois, do you have any identification?" asked Alister.

"Yes," he said. He reached into his pocket and withdrew his driver's license with its picture ID and handed it to Richard.

Richard read aloud, "Caspar DuBois. 42 years old. 5 feet, 8 inches in height. 150 pounds. Must wear eye glasses when driving." He returned the license to Mr. Dubois.

"Did you recognize your assailant, Mr. Dubois?" asked Alister.

"No. He had a mask on," answered Mr. Dubois.

"Actually, I think it was a ski mask, even though we are in late summer," added Mr. Dubois.

Alister said, "Mr. Dubois, please give us as detailed a description as you can of what happened."

"Well, I was asleep; it must have been about 1:00 AM when this happened. The robber might have come in that window," said Caspar, pointing to a window, "or maybe he had a key to the door. I've often wondered if the manager of this building always changes the locks on the doors when a new tenant moves in."

"So, you didn't hear him enter the room?" asked Alister.

"No, like I said, I was asleep. I almost always go to bed at about 11:00 PM," answered Caspar.

"Mr. Dubois, what do you do for a living?" asked Alister.

"I am a maintenance man in the Nelson building on Fifth Avenue," responded Caspar.

"Continue with your story Mr. Dubois. When were you first aware of the intruder?" asked Alister.

"I woke up to a sound I heard," answered Caspar. "He must have dropped something or accidentally kicked one of the legs of my bed. The couch here," pointing to a couch up against the wall, "opens up into a bed."

"I said, 'Who are you?' and he turned and jumped me. I was still groggy with sleep, so he had the original advantage. I was still under the covers, so that gave him another advantage."

"Did he say anything?" asked Alister.

"He made some kind of exclamation. I can't remember what."

"Go on with your testimony about what happened," said Alister.

"Well I finally got out from under the covers so I could fight better. I think I yelled 'Help' but I don't think anybody heard me. I landed one good punch on him and he fell to the floor. It was dark in the room; I guess he had been using a flash light. He got hold of something hard and heavy and hit me on the left side of my jaw with it. It might have been that book end over there on the floor. I keep it on the lower shelf of that book case."

"That really knocked me down and gave him the advantage," said Caspar. "I wasn't unconscious, though. I saw him pick up a bag of something off the dresser. Then he pulled the venetian blinds up on the window, yanked the window up, and climbed out. There is a fire escape outside the window. I guess he used that to get to the ground."

"Could you see him well enough to identify him?" asked Alister. "I guess it was pretty dark in here."

"I couldn't see his face; he had some kind of mask on," said Caspar. "It looked like a ski mask."

"How was he dressed? What size was he?" asked Alister.

"He had on a dark-colored jacket and dark colored pants," answered Caspar. "I think he was wearing athletic running shoes. He seemed to be about 6 feet tall and was of about average weight for that height."

"Did you get up off the floor and look out the window soon enough after he left to see if he got into a car and drove away?" asked Alister.

"I did get to the window soon enough to see him jump from the fire escape to the alley. He ran out of the alley to the left onto the sidewalk. I didn't see him get into a car."

"What did you do then?" asked Alister.

"I considered calling 911 immediately," answered

Caspar, "but my jaw was bleeding some and my shoulder hurt. I decided to go to the clinic on Fourth Avenue and Pine Street. They are open 24 hours a day. There is a doctor and a nurse during the day, but only a nurse at night. I figured I would call 911 from there."

"Have you noticed yet what has been stolen?" asked Alister.

"So far, I have discovered that he took about $40.00 from my wallet, and also my new wrist watch," answered Caspar.

Alister said, "After the forensic team has been here and left, you can continue your search. If you discover that something else is missing you can reach me at this number."

Alister gave Dubois his police department card with his name and phone number on it.

"All right. Richard, you take his statement while I look around," said Alister.

Alister stepped to the door and then turned to get a good overall view of the room. The apartment consisted of one fairly large room with a bathroom and a closet. The main room was partitioned into a kitchen space, an eating space, and a living room space. The partition consisted of a wooden frame that was attached to the floor and ceiling. The wood frame held brown plastic panels that depicted forest scenes. The kitchen contained an electric stove and a refrigerator. There was a sink and countertop against one wall. At one end of the partition was an eating area consisting of a small table and three chairs. The rest of the room constituted the living room.

Alister opened the closet door and looked in. There was a hot water heater and several shelves. Clothes could be hung on a 4 foot long horizontal clothes hanging rod. Caspar DuBois had hung several coats and jackets on the clothes rod. There were also numerous shirts and trousers on the clothes rod. Two pairs of shoes were on the floor.

Alister gazed back into the living room. It held a studio couch. When it was closed, it became a reddish brown colored couch. When it was open, it became the bed. Dubois hadn't closed it into a couch today because of the robbery last night. The three cushions were stacked on the floor and the couch was in the pulled out position. The bedsheets were rumpled and lying partly on the floor. The pillow was on the floor.

The drapes were drawn at the window. Dubois apparently wanted to leave the room like it was right after the robbery. The drapes were of a heavy light brown colored material. A second window was on another wall. This window was slightly open. Dubois said this was the window the intruder used to enter and leave the apartment. Alister stepped over to this window and looked out. Right outside the window was a black steel fire escape that led to the alley below. Dubois' apartment was on the second floor.

Alister looked back into the room. It was dimly lit at this point since the drapes were still drawn. However, the ceiling light was turned on. The rug was a medium brown colored shag rug. The walls were the daubed plaster type, painted a light beige color.

Due to the robbery and scuffle last night, a number of things lay scattered on the floor. Two chairs were knocked over. A book case had been knocked over and books were scattered on the carpet. A lamp was lying on the floor. A bureau against one wall had most of its drawers pulled out. The drawers appeared to be lying upside down on the floor.

Alister walked over and stooped to look at a book end that was lying on the rug next to the books that had fallen to the floor when the book shelf had been tipped over in the scuffle. Alister thought this was the object used by the intruder to strike Dubois during the scuffle. Alister didn't touch it. He would wait until the forensics team had checked it for fingerprints and blood drops.

Alister went over to the bureau and knelt down to examine the objects lying on the floor. It appeared that the bureau had not been knocked over in the fight, but rather that the intruder had taken all the drawers except the top drawer out and placed them on the floor. Presumably, he then went systematically through the drawers looking for something to steal.

Alister decided that after forensics completes its check of the bureau items for fingerprints, he will direct DuBois to go through the bureau's contents to see what is missing.

Alister checked the floor carefully for any pieces of torn clothing or ripped off buttons that could have resulted from the fight. He didn't notice anything in particular.

Alister moved to the window leading to the fire escape. He could see that the window had been forced open from the outside. It might have been pried up from the outside with a bar of some type, like a crowbar. That would have kept the break-in quiet. Striking the window from the outside would have awakened anyone sleeping inside.

Alister examine the window sill. He wanted to see if anything fell off the intruder's shoes on his way in or out. He couldn't spot anything.

Alister decided that before he left he would inspect the alley to see if the intruder might have dropped something on his way out.

The couch was still in the bed configuration. Caspar DuBois had not made the bed and returned the bed to the couch configuration. Cushions were stacked on the floor and the sheets were still rumpled on the bed. The top sheet was on the floor attesting to DuBois' claim that the fight or struggle had started on the bed.

Alister checked the floor of the room, looking for anything that the assailant might have dropped on the floor during the scuffle. Alister noticed a small dark object on the floor in front of the bureau and stooped to look at it carefully. It appeared to be a black button that came from a jacket or outer coat. Alister didn't pick it up or touch it. He wrote in his notebook to tell the photographer to take a picture of it when he arrived with the fingerprint man. Alister would call in the forensics team in a few minutes.

Alister put on a pair of latex gloves and turned his attention to the bureau. All of the drawers except the top drawer were pulled out and were lying on the floor. The contents of the drawers was all jumbled. He didn't know if that was due to Caspar DuBois' lack of tidiness or the assailant's searching efforts.

On top of the bureau was a receipt from Emerald City Diamond for the purchase of the new wrist watch. Alister moved on.

A chair and a lamp were on the floor. Alister noticed an object a little larger than a book lying on the floor near the bed. When he stooped to examine it, it appeared to be a book end. Alister didn't touch or move it. He made another note in his notebook to have the object first photographed in situ and then checked for fingerprints.

Alister next moved to the bathroom. The room was a mess. A bath towel had been thrown on top of the toilet tank. The toilet had not been flushed. A toothbrush was lying in the sink.

Alister opened the medicine cabinet and noticed an assortment of aspirin, Tylenol, and other pain relievers. There was also a small bag of marijuana. Alister left the bathroom thinking that Caspar DuBois was not a very tidy or clean person.

Chapter 2

When Alister stepped out of the bathroom, Richard was just completing Caspar DuBois' statement. Alister got out his cell phone and called into headquarters to request a forensics team.

"Caspar DuBois," said Alister, "I don't want you to touch or move anything until the forensics team gets here. I just called them in."

"OK," said Caspar.

"Let's talk about your movements and conversations the past few days," said Alister.

"What do you want to know?" asked Caspar. He seemed apprehensive for the first time.

"Let's start with your purchase of the new wrist watch," said Alister.

"I bought the new watch at Emerald City Diamond on Fourth Avenue near University Street," said Caspar.

"In addition to new watches and jewelry, that place has some secondhand jewelry to sell," said Caspar.

"So, do you think that jewelry stores buy second hand jewelry at auctions?" asked Alister.

"Sure," answered Caspar.

"When did you buy your new wrist watch?" asked Alister.

"I saw it in the window at Emerald City Diamond about three weeks ago. I didn't have the money until about two weeks later," answered Caspar.

"Let's see, that would've been September 5th," continued Caspar.

"Do you receive a monthly check from Social Security?" asked Alister.

"No. You have to be at least 62 to get Social Security," said Caspar. "I receive a State health disability check every month. I am allowed to work part time and receive the check. It usually arrives the fourth of every month."

"So, you went the next day to buy your wrist watch?" asked Alister.

"Yes," responded Caspar.

"Did you show it to your friends or talk about it much?" asked Alister.

"Well, I showed it to some of my friends when I got back from the store," answered Caspar.

"Where were you when you showed your new wrist watch to people?" asked Alister.

"Well, up here in my room for one place. And downstairs in our sitting room for another place," responded Caspar.

"What are the names of the people you spoke to?" asked Alister.

"Let's see. There was David Simmons and Charles Wilson in my room and several others in our sitting room," responded Caspar.

"Where do these people live?" asked Alister.

"They all live in this building," answered Caspar.

"So, did they admire your new watch?" asked Alister.

"Of course. They thought it was beautiful. David Simmons asked how much it cost," responded Caspar.

"Did you tell him?" asked Alister.

"Yes. I'd told him it cost $225," answered Caspar DuBois.

"So, you just showed them your new watch," said Alister, "and they expressed an admiration for it I suppose."

"Yes," said Dubois, "and we also talked some about the new operating system I bought recently for my old computer. I had Operating System 5 on my old computer and I recently bought Operating System 6 and installed it on my old computer. I was having trouble running the new operating system."

"Did you think your friends could help you?" asked Alister.

Dubois answered, "Yes. I have been using my old computer, which I have had for years, as a conversational piece. I showed off my brand new wrist watch while running my computer."

"You use your computer as a conversational piece? What do you usually talk about?" asked Alister.

"Well," answered Caspar, "I talk about difficulties I have with the operating system or things on the Internet. I ask my friends for help in overcoming these difficulties."

"So, during these conversations about computer operating system difficulties, your friends noticed your new wristwatch. Is that the case?" asked Alister.

"Yes," answered Dubois.

"Did your friends succeed in overcoming your operating system difficulties?" asked Alister.

"Yes, they did. A lot of my friends have been using Operating System 6 for years and they are proficient in its use," answered Dubois.

"Did you show your new watch to anybody else?"

"I took it with me over to Arnold's Broiler one night. I met Janet Smith and Charlene Heath and Jennifer Worthington there and we talked about my new watch some," said Caspar. "They thought it was great."

"I had gone down to Arnold's Broiler to get something to eat. I had taken along my old computer to use the Wi-Fi there," continued Caspar.

"I just happened to meet Janet Smith there," said Caspar.

"Where does she live?" asked Alister. "Do you know?"

"Janet lives in the Morley building on Fifth Avenue," responded Caspar. "Janet and I have been dating for almost a year now."

"Did you and Janet talk about your new watch and computer?" asked Alister.

Dubois answered, "Janet and I talked some about my new watch and also about my computer problems. As I said, I am fairly proficient in the use of Operating System 5 but I'm not very good at my new operating system, Operating System 6."

"Did you notice if any other patrons in the restaurant were listening to your conversation about your computer or new watch?" asked Alister.

"Well, there were other patrons in the restaurant but I don't know if they were paying any attention to us," answered Caspar.

Alister decided to turn the conversation back to Caspar DuBois' room where they were sitting.

"Did you look around this room, that we are now sitting in, after you returned from the clinic to see if anything else was missing?" asked Alister.

"Yes, I looked some but didn't notice anything else missing in addition to the wrist watch. Of course, if we had not had our fight he might have stolen other things," said Caspar.

Alister said, "I noticed when I walked into this building that there is a sitting room, or sort of living room, just inside the front door on the first floor."

"Yes. That is our sitting room where we can go and visit with the other tenants in this building," responded Caspar.

"Did you talk to anyone down there about your new wrist watch?" asked Alister.

"Oh, yes. Several times, actually."

"Do you recall the names of those you spoke to?" asked Alister.

"Well, I spoke to Dolores Jones and one night I spoke to Ralph Jenkins down there," answered Caspar.

Alister wrote the names down in his notebook. He realized that he would have to interview them later. Alister changed the subject slightly.

"While you were giving your statement to Richard a few minutes ago, I looked around your apartment some."

"OK," responded Caspar.

"I noticed that the top drawer of your bureau over there," continued Alister while pointing to a medium-sized brown bureau on the wall to the left, "was open. Inside the drawer is a box that contains some cuff links, a tie clasp, and a few other things. There is a wrist watch band but no wristwatch. I would like for you to look at the box and decide if anything is missing."

"Be careful not to touch anything; just look at them without touching them. I want the forensics team to examine everything for fingerprints."

"OK," said Caspar.

Caspar got up and went to the bureau and looked into the already opened top drawer.

"My new wrist watch was stolen from this watch band. I had an old watch attached to this old watch band for years, but I put my new watch in the watch band when I bought it recently. I put the old watch in a little box in the drawer; it is probably still here."

"What kind of watch was the old one?" asked Alister.

"It is a gold plated wrist watch; it's about five years old," answered Caspar.

"The watch has a scratch on the back of it in the shape of two nearly parallel lines," continued Caspar.

Alister recorded these remarks in his notebook. He said, "Caspar, why don't you look carefully at the rest of the bureau and see if anything else is missing. Make sure you don't touch anything."

Dubois knelt down to examine the bureau's drawers that the intruder had placed on the floor. After a minute, Dubois looked up and exclaimed, "My ring is gone."

He started hunting more earnestly through the things on the floor with a pencil to avoid smudging any finger prints that the intruder might have left. After a couple of minutes he said, "Yes, my ring is gone. I have always kept it here in this bureau drawer."

Alister asked, "What kind of ring was it?"

Dubois answered, "It was a silver ring with a green emerald inset. I received it from my aunt eight years ago."

Alister wrote this information in his notebook and asked, "Were there any unique distinguishing markings on it? There might be a lot of silver rings with green emerald insets out there."

Dubois sat for a moment and thought. He said, "I had my initials engraved on the inside of the ring band years ago. My initials are 'CMD'."

Alister recorded this in his notebook and asked, "Anything else missing?"

Dubois looked at the things on the floor and said, "I don't think so."

Alister said, "Maybe your assailant was going through your bureau drawers when you woke up."

Caspar moved around in front of the bureau looking carefully but not touching anything. "Things are rearranged but nothing else seems to be missing."

At this moment a knock occurred on the door and Alister's forensic team walked in. Alister said, "The forensics team is here. Let's step out into the hall and give them an opportunity to inspect the apartment for evidence." He looked at Richard and Caspar and said, "Maybe we could go down to the first floor and talk. The forensics team will need about an hour."

The three of them left the room and took the stairs down. There was a bench against the wall on the first floor next to the staircase.

"Let's sit here and talk," Alister said.

The hallway led from the staircase to the front door. Just inside the front door to the right of the hallway was a large room. Two couches and five chairs were in the room. Two tables with newspapers on them were before the couches. Four men were sitting in the chairs and looking at Caspar and the detectives when they came down the stairs.

Caspar said, "The tenants come down to this sitting room from their rooms to visit. A lot of us work nights and come down here during the day."

"Where did you say you worked; you told me before and I wrote it down?" asked Alister.

"I am a maintenance man in the Nelson building on Fifth Avenue," answered Caspar.

"You were attacked in your room Thursday night," remarked Alister. "Did you have that night off?"

"I have Monday, Wednesday, and Fridays off. I only work part time," answered Caspar.

"Did you talk to anyone at work about your new wrist watch?" asked Alister.

"Yes," answered Caspar.

"Have you taken your new watch to work and shown it around?" asked Alister.

"Oh, yes," answered Caspar.

"I have a few times but not often," continued Caspar.

"You said that you receive a State or Federal monetary allowance," said Alister.

"I receive a State monthly check for a health condition," answered Caspar. "Several of the tenants in my building do."

"The State forwards housing allowance and food assistance to a lot of men and women," said Alister. "And, those checks go out during the first few days of every month."

"Yes, I know," replied Caspar. "I suppose the thieves in

this area know that a lot of people in this poor area have extra money the first week of every month."

"Maybe, your assailant broke into your apartment on the fifteenth of the month to steal what you bought with your money, not the money, itself," said Alister.

"Yes, he might have known that I get monetary assistance from the State government," said Caspar.

At that point, the forensics team came down the stairs and told Alister that they were through and they would have their report on his desk the next morning.

Alister stood up and Richard also got up.

"We will be going now," Alister said to Caspar. "You can return to your room."

When they got to their car, Alister said to Richard, "I want to just check the alley for a few minutes. The intruder might have dropped something."

Richard said, "He might have. But a lot of other people might have dropped something too."

Alister responded, "Yes, of course that is true. But the intruder might have dropped something that reveals his identity. That way we will have the name of one more person to interview."

They walked around the building and entered the alley. After finding the fire escape and figuring out which window was Caspar DuBois', they started looking on the ground.

Alister said, "Dubois said he looked out the window and saw the robber leave the alley and go around that building."

Alister pointed at a building at the end of the alley. They checked the alley carefully from the fire escape to the building on the corner of the alley. They checked the ground immediately under the fire escape very carefully because something might have come out of the thief's pocket when he jumped from the fire escape to the ground.

After about twenty minutes, Richard said, "I don't think we're going to find anything."

Alister responded, "Yes, I think you are right. It was just worth checking out."

CHAPTER 3

He paused a minute and said, "Let's go," and headed out of the alley.

Richard and Alister left the alley and got into their car. "Let's get back to the office and plan our interviews with the people Caspar DuBois told us about," said Alister.

"We don't have much to go on," said Richard. "Just the people he talked to about his new watch and the problem he was having with a new operating system on his old computer. There is also the missing silver ring with green emerald inset. There wasn't much money to entice anyone."

"We probably won't be on the case very long," responded Alister. "There are murders in this city every month. The department won't spend much time and money on aggravated assault and robbery. But we will have to question all the leads we have."

When they got back to the police station they left the car in the basement garage and took the elevator to the third floor. They entered the squad room and went to their cubicle. They hung their jackets on the coat tree and put their guns back in their desk drawers.

Alister checked to see if he had any calls on his phone and found none.

"Do you want to go down to the lobby and get some coffee at the coffee stand?" asked Richard.

"Sure, why not," returned Alister.

They took the elevator down and walked to the coffee stand. Margaret was working at the stand. "Hi," she said. "How are things going with you two today?"

"Hello, Margaret. Everything is great. Thank you. I'll have a cappuccino," said Richard.

"Hello, Margaret," said Alister. "I'll have an Americano."

When they were served, Alister said, "Let's sit over there by the window for a few minutes."

They sat in the coffee bar and looked out the window for a while.

"How do you want to start this?" asked Richard.

"Well, I guess we will have to start with the people that Dubois spoke to," answered Alister. "We will interview them and see what develops."

"We can also check with the pawn shops on First Avenue in a couple of days to see if the new wrist watch or silver ring turns up," suggested Richard.

"I'll speak to James Newton in forensics this afternoon to see if anything turned up in their search of Dubois' apartment after we left," said Alister.

After a pause, Alister went on, "Why don't you start by compiling a list of the pawn shops we can visit on First Avenue, downtown, and also on Marginal Way out by SeaTac airport. I'll start with the health clinic on Fourth and Pine. Maybe they have a bloody cloth that Dubois had wrapped his hand in when he showed up at their clinic this morning. We might get some DNA."

"OK, so today is Thursday the 15th, the day of the crime.

Tomorrow, Friday, we can start interviewing the people DuBois spoke to during the past week or two," said Richard.

"Right," said Alister. "You could interview the people at DuBois' residence and I'll interview the people at Arnold's Broiler."

"They finished their coffees and went up to their office. After checking their email and phone call records, they set out. They agreed to meet at the office at 5:00 PM to compare notes.

When Alister entered the 24 hour clinic on Fourth Avenue and Pine, he went up to the receptionist. He showed his badge and said, "I am investigating a case that involves a man who came in here about 2:00 AM this morning. His name is Caspar DuBois."

The receptionist looked carefully at his badge and then turned to her computer to find the record of Dubois' visit. After a few moments she said, "Mr. Dubois checked in here at 2:20 AM this morning. The nurse on duty at that time was Alice Smith."

She looked around for a moment and then said, "She is with a patient right now. If you will sit over there," nodding at some chairs, "I will tell her you are here as soon as she is free."

Alister went to the chairs and sat down. He noticed several people sitting there awaiting their turn. After about 20 minutes a nurse came up to him and asked, "Alister Jensen? My name is Alice Smith."

Alister stood up and showed her his badge. "I am detective Alister Jensen of the Seattle Police Department. I would like to ask you a few questions about a patient you tended to this morning."

"All right," responded Alice. "Let's go to an office this way, please." She gestured towards the rear of the clinic and led the way.

When they entered a vacant office, nurse Alice started by saying, "I am not allowed to discuss some things about patients. But perhaps I can help you some."

Alister Jensen began, "Yes, I know there are privacy regulations." He took out his notebook and paged through it for second. He continued, "We spoke to Caspar DuBois at his apartment this morning. He said he came here with an injured jaw and back after he had a fight with somebody during the night."

"Yes. The left side of his jaw had been struck by a solid object," said nurse Smith. "The skin was bruised and his jaw will be sore for some time. But he didn't lose any teeth. We performed an x-ray of his back and determined that he probably fell on some blunt object on the floor during the scuffle. No ribs were broken however." She paused and waited as Alister wrote these things in his notebook.

"You say," began Alister, "that he had a cut on his jaw. Did you notice any other blood on him, like on his shirt or hands?"

"There was some blood on his hands and some on his shirt," answered Alice Smith. "I wiped it off and threw the cloth in the sanitary disposal container."

"Do you still have that container?" asked Alister.

"Yes, we do," answered Alice. "The incident you refer to occurred only about seven hours ago. So, we haven't dumped or burned the garbage yet."

"I wonder if the police department could have that

material," said Alister. "I would like to send it to our labs for DNA analysis."

"You can have it," responded nurse Alice. "But bear in mind that there is refuse from several patients in there, not just from Caspar DuBois."

"Yes, I understand," said Alister.

She left the room for a few minutes and returned with a plastic bag. "I should have a receipt for this transaction," she said.

Alister reached in his suit coat pocket, retrieve a police form, filled it in, and signed it. He handed her the form. He said, "I know you're busy here and I won't keep you more than a few more minutes."

She nodded her consent, and Alister continued, "I would like for you to describe his manner and deportment and also anything he said that you can remember." Alister had his notebook and pen ready.

Alice began, "Well, he was very intense and agitated. But that is customary for anyone who has just sustained an injury. I looked at him and asked, 'How did this happen?' I could see that he was conscious and capable of talking. He said that he had been robbed and beaten. So, I asked him if he wanted me to call the police. He said, 'No. I'll call them later when I leave.' I said, 'Did you get stabbed or shot?' I started looking at his shirt and pants. He said, 'No. I just got hit a couple times. But, I hit him back a couple of times, too.' I asked him if he got a good look at his assailant. He said that he didn't get much of a look because the guy who attacked him had a mask on. So, I bandaged his jaw and we went to the x-ray room and took two x-rays of his back. The x-ray technician said there were no broken bones. So, Mr. Dubois got ready to leave."

Alister asked, "Did he mention where the struggle occurred or anything the robber said?"

"Mr. Dubois said that the attack occurred in his room during the night. He thought the robber came in through the window," answered Alice.

She thought a little more and then said, "He thought the robber said, during the fight, 'Where is your watch and money?'"

Alister said, "The cut on his jaw. Could that have been made by a ring on the robber's hand?"

"It could have," answered Alice. "But Mr. Dubois said that he thought that the cut was made by an embossed design on a porcelain or marble book end that was on the floor near his book case. He discovered it after the assailant left."

Alister stood and said, "Thank you for your time and help, nurse Smith. You have been helpful."

Nurse Alice Smith rose and walked with Alister to the door of the 24 hour clinic.

Alister took the bag of soiled bandages over to the forensics lab on Rainier Avenue. When he entered, he went to the fourth floor and proceeded to Ralph Lee's office. Ralph was not in his office, so Alister went to the labs on the third floor. He finally spotted Ralph in the lab seated at the electron microscope.

Alister knocked on the door and entered. When Ralph looked up, Alister held up his bag and said, "Hi, Ralph, I got something for you."

Ralph turned in his seat, gave a big smile and said, "Alister. Good to see you. Come on in."

Alister walked over and put the bag on a vacant table nearby. He said, "I've got some soiled bandages here from the 24 hour clinic on Fourth and Pine. One of the bandages in here is from Caspar DuBois. I'll send over his DNA sample later today. What I am interested in is whether you can find some other person's DNA on the same bandages that Alister Dubois' blood is on. The rest of the bandages don't interest me."

"OK," answered Ralph. "So, should I wait until I receive a sample of Caspar DuBois' blood or DNA from you later?"

"Yeah, I'll get a blood sample from him this afternoon, and send it over," said Alister.

"If we are able to find someone else's blood on Caspar DuBois' bandages, we will send it into the national DNA database CODIS. To get a response can take several days though," added Ralph.

"That's fine," said Alister. "We have a lot of witnesses to interview."

"Have you people received any new multimillion dollar equipment lately?" asked Alister with a grin on his face. "I know you people have fancy lab equipment."

"As a matter of fact, we have," said Ralph. We bought a DNA analyzer from Applied Biosystems. You introduce a specimen of blood into a well or receptacle on the machine and the machine generates an electropherogram. The machine uses primers to initiate the polymerase chain reaction that causes the DNA to replicate itself. The machine analyzes ten to fourteen loci; each locus has two alleles, one from the mother and one from the father. The computer software assigns numbers to each allele. The loci show up as peaks on the electropherogram strip. The presence of contamination, or other person's blood, shows up as peaks with noticeably different heights."

"So, you can compare two drops of blood, one from a crime scene and one from a national blood sample bank maintained by the FBI to try and identify the other person on the blood sample that came from the crime scene," said Alister.

"Right," responded Ralph. "We only have to send DNA material or analyses to Washington for the CODIS comparison when we have only blood from the crime scene."

"Well, I'll leave you to your work," said Alister. He stood and left the room.

Alister got into his unmarked police car and drove to the police station. When he got to his cubicle, Richard was there working on his list of pawn shops to visit.

Alister said, "I took some of DuBois' bandages from the 24 hour clinic to forensics to check for DNA."

"I've put together some likely pawn shops on First Avenue, downtown, and also some on Marginal Way out by the airport," said Richard.

"I suppose there is nothing else to do today. Tomorrow we start our interviews," said Alister.

With that, they put on their jackets and left.

Alister arrived at the squad room 8:00 am Friday morning, September 16th. Richard was already in their cubicle. "Hi, Alister," Richard said. "Today, we start our interviews."

"I am going over to Arnold's Broiler to see if I can find

anyone that Dubois talked to and showed them his new wrist watch," said Alister.

"OK," answered Richard. "I will be leaving shortly to talk to the people at DuBois' apartment house."

Alister decided to walk to Arnold's Broiler. It is on the corner of Third and Stewart and that is only about eight blocks from the police station. It was a pleasant day for a walk. Arnold's Broiler consists of essentially two rooms: a barroom and a restaurant. The restaurant has a counter in addition to quite a few booths.

When Alister stepped into the restaurant he noticed that there weren't many customers. He knew that Arnold's Broiler has a large clientele for lunch and supper for people who work downtown. It is also a favorite relaxation spot in the evening for people who live in the high rise condos downtown.

Alister walked up to the cashier and showed his badge to the girl behind the cash register. She wore a nameplate with the name Helen on it. "I am investigating Caspar DuBois' robbery," he said. "I would like to interview any of his friends that he typically meets here. Are there any here now?"

Helen looked at his badge and then took a glance around the room. "Charlene Heath, the girl sitting over by the window, is one of his friends," said Helen.

Alister walked over to the table where Charlene was sitting. She was wearing a white blouse with pink trim and blue jeans. She was reading a paperback. Alister couldn't tell if it was a novel or a book devoted to some current topic of interest. "Hello, Charlene. My name is Alister Jensen. I am a police detective doing a routine investigation of

Caspar DuBois' robbery. He told me that you were one of his friends. Could I sit down and speak to you for a few minutes?"

Charlene looked at his badge and said, "I suppose it is all right, and gestured towards the empty chair at her table."

Alister sat down. He began, "Caspar told me that he bought a new wrist watch a week or two ago and came in here and showed it to his friends." Alister took out his notebook and leafed through it. "He said he showed it to you and Janet Smith one night."

"Yes," responded Charlene. "Actually, there were three of us sitting together when Caspar came walking in with his new wrist watch. Janet Smith, Jennifer Worthington, and me."

Alister added Jennifer Worthington to the list he had in his notebook. "About how long did you people talk about his new watch?" asked Alister.

"Oh, about half an hour," answered Charlene.

"About what time of the day was it?" asked Alister. "Do you remember?"

"Oh, about 9:00 PM I think," answered Charlene.

Alister was writing her answers and responses in his notebook. "Did you notice if anyone at the adjacent tables was paying any attention to your conversation?"

"Several people glanced our way a few times," said Charlene. "A lot of people admire wrist watches. But no one paid much attention." She paused a moment and then corrected herself, "As a matter of fact, Siegfried Stone did come over and say something. I think he said something like, "Did you get a new watch, Caspar?" Then he sat down with us for a while."

Alister asked, "Does Siegfried Stone have a watch of his own?"

"I never noticed if Siegfried had a watch," answered Charlene. She paused for a moment and then continued, "I suppose Siegfried came over just to visit."

Alister wrote Siegfried Stone in his notebook. He asked, "Does Siegfried Stone frequent this place?"

"Oh, yes," answered Charlene. "He is frequently here."

"Is he here now?" asked Alister.

Charlene looked around, and said, "No. I don't see him. He comes in later."

"When does Janet Smith come by?" asked Alister, looking at his watch.

"She usually makes supper at home and then comes in later, maybe 7:00 PM," answered Charlene.

"Seven o'clock," repeated Alister, looking at his watch. "It's 4:10 pm now. Could you give me her address?"

"Well, I suppose I can," answered Charlene. "She lives in the Morley building on Fifth Avenue, Room 402. She works until 4:30 or 5:00 PM at one of the downtown department stores."

"And, Jennifer Worthington. When does she come in?" asked Alister.

"She is usually here by now," answered Charlene. "I don't know where she is." Charlene turned in her seat and looked around. "Oh, there she is," she said. "She is the girl in the green jumper sitting by herself over there in the corner." Charlene nodded in the direction of a girl in the far corner.

Alister said, "Thank you for your help Miss Heath. I think that will be all for now." He stood and said, "Perhaps I can speak briefly to Jennifer Worthington before I leave."

Alister moved to the table in the corner where Jennifer Worthington was sitting. She was an attractive dark haired girl dressed in a green suit. When Alister approached her table, he said, "Hello Ms. Worthington. My name is Alister Jensen. I am a Seattle police detective investigating the robbery of Caspar DuBois."

Alister showed her his badge. She looked closely at it. Alister continued, "I am conducting routine interviews with the friends and acquaintances of Caspar DuBois. May I ask you a few questions?"

She said, "Yes, that would be all right. Why don't you sit there," gesturing towards a chair at her table.

Alister sat.

She began, "I noticed Charlene Heath at the window when I came in. Ordinarily, I would have gone up to her and spoken to her. But I saw you talking to her and so decided not to intrude."

Alister took out his notebook and opened it. He said, "Charlene Heath mentioned to me that you and she and Janet Smith were sitting in here one night about a week ago when Caspar DuBois came in."

"Yes," said Jennifer. "He came up to us and showed us his wrist watch which he had recently bought."

Alister said, "I suppose you all exclaimed how beautiful his new watch was."

"Yes, we certainly did," said Jennifer.

"Did you notice if any other patrons in the restaurant paid much attention to you?" asked Alister.

"Well, no one paid much attention. Siegfried Stone came over after a while and joined in our conversation," said Jennifer.

"Do you recall anything he said?" asked Alister.

"Oh, he just asked Caspar how long he had had the watch and how much it cost," said Jennifer. "I think Caspar said he had just bought it and that it had cost $225," she went on.

Alister recorded these things in his notebook and then said, "Thank you Jennifer Worthington. I think that will be all for now." Alister closed his notebook and stood. He smiled and left.

Chapter 4

Alister left Arnold's Broiler and headed up Third Avenue. He looked at his watch and decided that he had about an hour before Janet Smith would be home from work. So he went over to the Randolph's Coffee Shop on Fifth Avenue for a coffee. He got an Americano and sat at a window overlooking the sidewalk. Alister thought to himself that he had nothing so far except the statement from Charlene that Siegfried Stone took an interest in the new wrist watch and invited himself over to the table where Caspar DuBois, Charlene, and Janet were sitting to ask questions. Nothing much to that thought Alister, but he entered it into his notebook. Alister took out his cell phone and called his partner, Richard Hopkins.

After four rings, Richard answered, "Richard, here."

Alister said "Richard, I'll be at the office a little after five. I am going over to Janet Smith's apartment to talk to her. She works until 4:30 or 5:00 o'clock."

"Okay," answered Richard. "I'll see you at the office."

Alister closed his cell phone and sat for a while longer watching the crowd. Finally, he got up and went out. When he got to the Morley building he noticed it was just 5:15. Alister wasn't sure that the building' door on the walkway leading to the Fifth Avenue sidewalk would be open. He figured it would be open during the day and locked at night. Since it was 5:15 PM he decided to give it a try. He walked up to the door and found it unlocked. He entered the foyer and found Janet Smith's name next to her mailbox on the wall. It was room 402. He could push the button next to her name on her mailbox and talk to her over the adjacent microphone speaker. But he decided to walk up the staircase and knock on her door. Alister went up to room 402 and knocked on the door.

Janet Smith answered after a few minutes. She put the chain on the door and opened it about an inch to look out. "Yes?" she said.

Alister showed her his badge and said he was a Seattle police detective investigating Caspar DuBois' robbery. He asked if he could come in and ask her a few questions.

Janet Smith reached through the door opening, around the chain, took his badge and took it inside her apartment to inspect it carefully. She finally decided that it looked genuine. She passed his badge back out and took the chain off the door.

"One can't be too careful about letting unfamiliar people into one's apartment," she said, opening the door.

"Thank you," said Alister, entering. "No, you have to be very careful," he said.

Janet Smith's apartment was brightly lighted by windows to the East. She had white lace curtains and the window shade was up. It was a nice change from the standard venetian blind style of the day.

"It's nice and airy and bright in here," said Alister.

"Yes," said Janet, with a smile. "I appreciate sunny pleasant days."

They walked over to the window and glanced out. It provided a view of the Convention Center, built over the north-south running Hwy 5. Turning around, Alister noticed a brown leather couch with matching chair in the living room.

Janet said, "The couch and chair were chosen by Caspar DuBois. We are engaged to be married and he offered to buy a new couch and chair if he got to choose them. They are very expensive."

Alister responded, "Yes, I know."

Janet went on, "If it had been my choice, I probably would have chosen one of the very attractive upholstered chairs they had on display at the furniture store."

Alister smiled and noticed a copy of one of Renoir's paintings on the wall. He said, "I suppose it is very convenient to live this close to work. You don't even have to drive to work."

"No, I walk," answered Janet. "I work at an upscale department store just four blocks from here."

Alister decided to direct the conversation to the purpose of his visit.

"Caspar DuBois gave me your name, Charlene's name and Jennifer Worthington' name. He said he spoke to you three at Arnold's Broiler and showed you his new wrist watch," said Alister.

"Yes," said Janet. "Caspar and I often meet at Arnold's Broiler. As I said before, we are engaged to be married. Charlene and Jennifer are good friends of mine."

Alister took out his notebook and leafed through it. "He

said he had bought a new wrist watch and showed it to you. He also said that he talked to you about a new operating system that he had bought for his old computer."

"Yes," answered Janet. "He showed me his new watch. It is beautiful. He also told me that he had bought a new operating system, Operating System 6, for his old computer and that he was having some trouble using it. His old computer came with Operating System 5. I was able to help him some because I have been using Operating System 6 for quite a while. Arnold's Broiler has Wi-Fi and Caspar had brought his computer along."

"While you were talking," continued Alister, "did anyone seem to pay any close attention. Charlene Heath mentioned that Siegfried Stone came over. Did anyone else pay attention or come over?"

"I remember that Siegfried came over and showed an interest. But that wasn't unusual. He is always around Arnold's Broiler. He didn't ask anything special. Siegfried just watched us while we surfed around some on the Internet. Siegfried was impressed by Caspar's new watch and expressed admiration for it."

"So, Siegfried Stone took an interest in Dubois' new wrist watch," said Alister. "Did he show much interest in the computer and what you were doing?"

"No, not really," answered Janet. "I don't even know if Siegfried Stone has a computer. I suppose he does. Everybody else does."

She went on after laughing a bit, "Caspar and I were surfing around on the Internet. I was showing Caspar how to use the menus and keys available in Operating System 6 to navigate on the Internet."

She paused a moment, and then continued, "Maybe Siegfried Stone was attracted by our talking about the Internet and came over to watch."

Alister asked, "While the three of you were running Caspar's old computer, did you notice if anyone else in the restaurant was watching you?"

"I didn't notice anybody," answered Janet, "but I suppose they heard us and noticed our attention riveted on the computer. Perhaps we were talking a little loud at times."

"Back again to the wrist watch," said Alister. "I guess a gold plated watch is a bit showy. Did Caspar DuBois flash it around sometimes?"

"Not really," answered Janet. "It is true that the watch is impressive looking, but I don't think Caspar flashed it about."

"Do you recall what time of day it was and what day it was?" asked Alister.

"Yes, I remember," said Janet, "It was Saturday of last week. And, it was around 7:00 PM. The reason I remember is because Alister and I had planned on going to the movies at 9:00 PM. There was a detective story on at the Bay theater."

Alister wrote this down in his notebook. It didn't seem germane to anything, but he wrote it down anyway. "So, about what time did you leave for the theater? Do you recall?" he asked.

"We left around 8:30 PM I think," answered Janet.

"When Siegfried Stone asked about Caspar DuBois' wristwatch, do you remember exactly what he asked?" went on Alister.

"I think he asked Caspar how much a new wrist watch

costs. He knew Caspar had just recently bought the watch," answered Janet.

"Had Caspar shown his new watch to several of his friends after he bought it?" asked Alister.

"Yes, I think so," answered Janet.

"Let's get on to the day of the robbery," said Alister. "Did you see Caspar DuBois that day? It was Thursday, September 15th," said Alister.

"Yes. Caspar and I had gone to the grocery store to buy some groceries and then we came home to my apartment to cook it," answered Janet.

"Do you recall when Mr. Dubois went home?" asked Alister.

"Well, not exactly. I guess it was around 11:00 PM. I had to go to work the next day," answered Janet.

"I suppose he was wearing his new watch," said Alister.

"Yes he was," answered Janet.

"So, you have to go to bed around 11:00 PM since you need to be a work at 9:00 AM the next morning, Janet Smith," said Alister. "But Caspar DuBois might not have to get up that early. Do you suppose he might have stopped into Arnold's Broiler that night for a drink or to say hello to his friends?" asked Alister.

"He might have," said Janet. "He does have several friends there. But he would have mentioned his intention of stopping there when he left here. But, he didn't mention that. So, I don't think he stopped at Arnold's."

Alister said, "I was just wondering if he might have encountered a potential thief on the way home. All right, Ms. Smith. That's all the questions I have at this time.

Perhaps I can speak to you again if something comes up," said Alister. He rose and moved toward the door.

Janet Smith accompanied him to the door. "Yes, I am available for any further questions. Caspar was not hurt badly. I am thankful for that," said Janet Smith. "Do you have any suspect yet?" she asked.

"It is still very early in the case," responded Alister. He said goodbye and left.

Alister decided to return to the police station. He recalled that he and Richard had decided yesterday to interview the friends and acquaintances of DuBois today, and discuss their interviews tomorrow, Saturday. Alister figured he could update his computer record of his three interviews today.

Chapter 5

Richard walked into the squad room early Friday morning, September 16th. It was just 8:05 AM. Several detectives were at their desks either getting caught up on their paperwork or planning out their day. Alister wasn't in their cubicle yet when Richard walked in.

He decided he would start with his interviews of the people at Caspar DuBois' building that Dubois had shown his new wrist watch to.

It was still pretty early and some of them might not be up yet. Richard decided to update his records of the day Alister and he had gone to speak to Caspar DuBois. At 9:30 AM Richard had completed his paperwork. Alister had not come in yet. Richard figured he was over at Arnold's Broiler interviewing the people there.

Richard put on his jacket and took his Glock 9 mm from his desk drawer. He put his gun in his under the arm holster and headed for the door. He took the elevator down to the first floor and went out the door onto Fourth Avenue.

The weather had been very nice the past couple of weeks, and therefore Richard decided to walk to Caspar DuBois' building. It was only a few blocks.

Richard didn't anticipate any difficulty getting into

Dubois' building. It was 9:45 AM on a workday morning, and he figured the main entrance to the building would be unlocked. When he got to Dubois' building at 1204 Third Avenue, the glass door was unlocked as he had expected.

Richard passed through the foyer and continued past a sitting room on the left on his way to the elevators. He assumed this sitting room was the one referred to by Dubois when he talked about conferring with his friends about his new watch or his computer. Richard checked to make sure his first interviewee was not sitting there now. Nobody was in the sitting room.

Richard checked his list of people to interview. David Simmons was in room 105. He decided to try Simmons first. Richard proceeded down the hall and found room 105. He checked his watch and found that it was just 10:00 AM. He knocked on the door. He heard a slight stirring inside the room and soon the door was opened.

David Simmons apparently had been sitting in his kitchen eating breakfast. He had on a white T-shirt and dark trousers. He was barefoot. He hadn't shaved or combed his hair yet. He looked to be about 35 years old.

He dabbed his mouth with a napkin and said, "Hello."

Richard said, "I am looking for Mr. David Simmons."

Simmons said, "I am David Simmons."

Richard Hopkins continued, "Mr. Simmons, I am detective Richard Hopkins of the Seattle police department. I am investigating the robbery of Caspar DuBois and I am conducting routine interviews with the people that Caspar DuBois said he spoke to concerning his new wrist watch. May I come in?"

David Simmons hesitated a second and then said,

"All right. I just got up a little while ago and I was eating breakfast in my kitchen. We can sit here in the living room and talk."

He scurried about straightening the papers and books on the tables in the room. He opened the venetian blinds at the window to let a little light in. David Simmons had a couch and matching chair. They were leather covered and quite nice. There was a rather large disk player in the room with what looked like a large and expensive speaker system. There was a book case against one wall.

Simmons asked, "Would you like some coffee? I just made some in the kitchen."

Richard answered, "Yes, thank you. That would be fine."

Simmons asked, "Milk and sugar?"

Richard answered, "Just black, please."

Moments later Simmons returned with two cups of coffee and saucers. He asked, "Will this take long? I can call into work and say that I am being interviewed by the police about the robbery of a friend of mine, and I will be in a little later."

Richard answered, "This is just a routine interview and will probably only take about 15 or 20 minutes."

Simmons said, "I'll just take a fast shave and shower when we are done. I will only be a few minutes late."

Richard began, "Where do you work, Mr. Simmons?"

Simmons answered, "I work as an accountant with Evergreen Office Consultants on Fourth Avenue."

Richard had his notebook out and was recording data.

"Have you been an acquaintance of Caspar DuBois for long?" asked Richard.

Simmons answered, "I have been living here for about two years, and met him when I first moved in."

Richard paged through his notebook and stopped at a page. "Caspar DuBois said that when he bought his new wrist watch a week or two ago, he showed it to you and several other people in the building. Do you recall that occasion?"

"Yes," answered Simmons. "He accosted me in the hallway one evening and mentioned that he had just bought a wrist watch. He showed me his new watch. It was very handsome".

"He just passed you in the hallway one night and brought this up?" asked Richard.

"Yes, he said that he knew that I was an accountant and used computers a lot. So, he thought maybe I could help him with a problem he had with his old computer," answered Simmons.

"So, did you agree to help him?" asked Richard.

"Yes, I had just come home from work," said Simmons, "and I was standing in the hallway talking to another tenant of our building, Charles Wilson, when DuBois came up to us and told us about his new watch and old computer. I thought I might be able to help with his computer problem. So, he took us up to his room where he had his old computer on a table."

"What did he say his difficulty with his computer was?" asked Richard.

"Well, Caspar DuBois' old computer had Operating System 5 as its operating system and Dubois had just bought Operating System 6 as a new operating system," answered Simmons, "and he wasn't familiar with Operating System 6."

"Was he stuck navigating around on the Internet?" asked Richard.

"Yes," answered Simmons, "his computer was actually stuck at an Internet site and was not responding to keyboard entries."

"Did he have an instruction guide or computer book to consult?" asked Richard.

"No," answered Simmons. "Instruction books don't come with new operating systems."

"The instruction books that do come when you buy a brand-new computer aren't much help," interjected Richard.

"Yes, I know," agreed Simmons.

"Did you finally get his computer unstuck; did you get it to run?" asked Richard.

"Yes," answered Simmons. "I have had Operating System 6 as the operating system on my computer for a long time and I understand it fairly well."

"I have a computer at home that runs Operating System 6," said Richard Hopkins.

"We use Operating System 6 on our computers at work to maintain our office records," said Simmons. "So, I know how to run Operating System 6 fairly well. Our accounting program, however, runs on an expensive computer and I don't know what operating system it uses."

"To change the subject back to Dubois' wrist watch," said Richard, "did he say where he bought it?"

"He said he bought it new at Emerald City Diamond on Fourth Avenue," answered Simmons.

"Did he say how much he paid for it?" asked Richard.

"I think he said $225," answered Simmons.

"Well, a $225 item will entice a thief," said Richard.

"Yeah, but to gamble on being caught for stealing $225 worth of merchandise and then go to jail for a year or more doesn't seem very sensible," said Simmons.

"No, it doesn't sound sensible," agreed Richard.

"What do you think a thief could sell it for if he decided to sell it?" asked Simmons.

"I imagine he could probably hock it for about $125.00," responded Richard.

"The first thing against stealing is the ethics of it. It is wrong to steal," said Simmons. "But, in addition, any job is going to pay more than $125 per week."

"Right," responded Richard. "Working in a grocery store pays a lot better than that."

"I agree," responded Simmons. "I have passed a lot of grocery stores and been in some where they had signs up saying Help Wanted."

"Sometimes, perhaps a grocery store will not hire someone with a bad work history," said Richard.

"You might be right," returned Simmons.

Richard folded his notebook and put it in his pocket. He rose and said, "Thank you, Mr. Simmons for your time and for the coffee. I'll leave now and let you finish getting ready for work."

Simmons rose and went to the door with him. He said, "Goodbye, detective Hopkins."

Richard walked down the hall to the foyer again and looked at his watch. It was just 10:40 AM. Richard decided to interview another acquaintance of DuBois that morning. He could return to the office for lunch after that.

Richard got out his list of interviewees and decided to interview Charles Wilson. That would leave Dolores Jones and Ralph Jenkins for the afternoon. Richard wondered if Alister was making any headway with the people he interviewed at Arnold's Broiler.

Richard got out his cell phone and called Alister. Alister answered on the third ring. "Jensen here."

"Hi, Alister. It's Richard here. I was just wondering if you are making any great headway on your interviews."

"No, not so far," answered Alister. "How about you?"

"Nothing much. I've spoken to David Simmons so far; he told me that Caspar DuBois and he had a conversation about DuBois' computer problems, and DuBois had shown him his new watch."

"Maybe we will get a break from the forensics people," said Alister. "The interviews might just tell us who knew Dubois and that he had bought a new wrist watch."

Chapter 6

Richard pressed the elevator button for the fourth floor. He found Charles Wilson's room, 401, all right. He knocked and listened. No answer, so he knocked again. He heard some activity inside and soon the door was opened.

The man who appeared said, "Hello, what can I do for you?"

Richard said, "I am Richard Hopkins of the Seattle police department investigating the robbery of Caspar DuBois. I'm looking for Charles Wilson."

The man who responded to Richard's knocking said, "I am Charles Wilson. What can I tell you?"

Richard said, "We're just doing routine interviews with the people that Caspar DuBois spoke to about his new wrist watch. May I come in and ask you a few questions?"

Charles Wilson said, "OK, come in," and held the door open.

Richard entered the apartment. It had the same floor plan as did Dubois' apartment and David Simmons' apartment. The drapes on the window were still drawn closed. So, it was slightly dim in the room and the lights were on.

Wilson stepped over to the window and drew the drapes

open. He said, "It just started raining today so it is kind of gloomy."

Richard looked out to the West. It was completely overcast and he could not see the Olympic Mountains. He did see a ferry plying its way up the Sound on its way to Bainbridge Island.

Charles Wilson had a light tan cushioned couch with a matching chair. He had a very nice table and six chairs. The grain of the wood showed clearly. There were two bookcases, both crammed full.

Wilson said, "Can I offer you some coffee or water? I just made the coffee."

Richard answered, "Water would be fine, thank you."

Charles Wilson went to the kitchen and soon returned with a glass of water for Richard and a cup of coffee for himself.

"Please seat yourself and be comfortable," said Wilson. Wilson sat in the easy chair and Richard took the couch.

Richard took out his notebook and began, "Are you employed, Mr. Wilson?"

Wilson answered, "Yes, I am a math teacher in the community college system in Seattle."

"Oh, that's impressive," said Richard. "Have you been teaching long?"

"About five years," answered Charles Wilson.

"I suppose there are quite a few failing grades in a college math course," said Richard.

"Yes, it is difficult material and a lot of the students don't seem to be interested in it," said Wilson. "It is required material and the students, who are not math majors, think they don't really need it. It's just a required course."

"I suppose it is difficult to make mathematics interesting or exciting to a sociology major," said Richard.

"Yes, you have to possess considerable pedagogical skills," said Charles.

"Do the students get to repeat a course that they have failed?" asked Richard.

"Yes," answered Charles. "Sometimes they repeat a course four or five times, it seems."

"Do you have classes today, Mr. Wilson?" asked Richard.

"Yes," answered Charles Wilson. "I have one afternoon class on Tuesdays and Thursdays and two classes on Mondays, Wednesdays, and Fridays."

"OK, I'll try not to detain you too long," said Richard, getting out his notebook. He began, "Mr. Wilson, have you known Caspar DuBois long?"

"I've known Caspar DuBois about four years," said Charles Wilson. "That is how long I have lived in this building."

Richard consulted his notebook and went on, "Mr. Dubois stated that he showed his new wrist watch to you and David Simmons in his room one day. Do you recall that occasion?"

"Yes," answered Wilson. "His new watch was very attractive. He was also having trouble with his computer and he encountered David Simmons and me in the hallway one day and asked if we could help him with his computer."

"Did you go to his room to help?" asked Richard.

"Yes, we went to Dubois' room," said Charles. "He had his computer on a table in the room, so we all sat down there and tried to get it to run."

"Are you very familiar with computers, Mr. Wilson?" asked Richard.

"Oh yes," answered Charles. "I have been a programmer for years. I worked at several companies as a programmer. Right now, I am teaching."

"What was wrong with Dubois' computer?" asked Richard.

"Nothing was wrong with the computer," answered Charles Wilson. "Dubois had just bought a new operating system, Operating System 6, and was not familiar with it. He had been using Operating System 5."

"So the two of you got Dubois straighten out on his new operating system. That was all that was wrong?" asked Richard.

"Yes, really, that's all there was to it," answered Charles.

"Is there some instruction book a person could buy at a bookstore that would help him learn the Operating System 6?" asked Richard.

"Yes, I've seen books at bookstores that instruct people in the use of Operating System 6," answered Charles Wilson.

Richard continued, "Did Caspar DuBois show you his new wrist watch?"

"Yes, he did. It's a beauty," answered Charles.

"Did Caspar tell you how much he paid for his new watch?" asked Richard.

"Yeah, he told us that it cost $225," answered Charles.

"I suppose that is incentive enough to commit robbery for some people," said Richard.

"The thief would have to hock it, though, to get money for it and I doubt he could hock it for more than $125," said Charles.

"Yes, that is what I heard," said Richard.

Richard continued, "Do you know if Dubois talked about his computer or his watch to other people in his apartment building?"

"Well, yes," answered Wilson. "I heard that he talked to some people in our sitting room about them."

Richard said, "I think I have them on my list of people to interview."

Richard folded his notebook and put his pen in his pocket. He said, "Thank you for your assistance, Mr. Charles Wilson. I greatly appreciate it. Perhaps I could contact you again if something comes up."

Richard rose and moved towards the door. Charles Wilson walked with him to the door and said, "Sure, I'll help if I can."

Richard walked down the hallway and out into the rain. He thought to himself, well, that's two of them. Two more to go. I wonder if I'm going to come up with anything useful. He decided to go back to the police station and have lunch.

When Richard got to the station, he headed up to the squad room. Alister was in the cubicle and they decided to have lunch in the cafeteria. They headed for the elevator. It was the lunch hour, so the cafeteria was filling up fairly rapidly. They went down the cafeteria line. Alister chose Chili and coffee and a roll. Richard chose the pork and beans dish and coffee.

They eventually found a table and sat down. "Not too much progress this morning with my interviews," began Richard. "I have two more this afternoon."

"I have one late this afternoon. It's Janet Smith, DuBois' fiancé. She works in a store during the day," said Alister.

After lunch, Alister and Richard returned to the squad room and went to their cubicle. Richard had interviewed David Simmons and Charles Wilson that morning. So, that left two more to interview this afternoon.

Richard took out his list of people to interview. He had written Dolores Jones and Ralph Jenkins as the two people Dubois had spoken to in the sitting room at their building.

Richard put on his jacket. He took his 9 mm Glock from his desk drawer and put it in the holster under his jacket. He checked that he had his notebook in a shirt pocket and then walked out of the squad room.

He took the stairs down to the first floor and headed for the door. Dubois' building was only five blocks away. He could easily walk it. It wasn't raining out. It was kind of overcast outside, but that sometimes blows away in the afternoon. At least, that had been the case the past week or so.

Dubois' building was on Third Avenue. There were always a lot of pedestrians scurrying about on the sidewalks on a weekday afternoon. Quite a few of them pay close attention to the latest fashion and clothing. A lot of the office buildings and downtown stores are on Fourth Avenue. Richard decided to walk down Fourth Avenue and then cross over to Third Avenue when he got near Dubois' building.

When Richard got to Union Street, he took it down to Third Avenue. He arrived at 1204 Third Avenue at 1:20 PM according to his watch. He entered the building and went to the elevators. He decided to visit Dolores Jones first and Ralph Jenkins second.

According to his list, Dolores Jones lived in apartment 406. Richard took the elevator to the fourth floor. The hallways were pretty well kept up. The halls had wood floors and a rug running down the center. The rug had a geometric pattern using several different colors. At the end of each hall was a window. There was a curtain at each window and a small table. Management had put a flower vase containing presumably artificial flowers on each table.

Richard found apartment 406, Dolores Jones' apartment, without any trouble. He heard music coming through the door. He thought Dolores might be listening to some disk of hers on her hi-fi system. He knocked on the door but heard no response. Realizing that she probably had her record player turned on pretty loud, he knocked again, a little harder. This time he heard footsteps approaching the door.

The door opened and Dolores said, "Yes?"

Richard answered, "My name is Richard Hopkins. I am a Seattle police detective assigned to Caspar DuBois' robbery." Richard showed her his badge.

Richard said, "I am looking for Dolores Jones."

Dolores responded, "I am she."

Richard said, "I am conducting routine interviews with the friends of Caspar DuBois. May I ask you a few questions?"

Dolores answered, "Yes. Come in." She opened the door wider.

Richard stepped into Dolores Jones' apartment. It was very cheerfully decorated. There were curtains at the windows. The shade was up and the windows open slightly so that the wind tossed the curtain about some. It was bright and airy in the room.

The couch was dark blue and had white doilies on the arms. Richard hadn't seen that in a long time. A matching chair was up against the adjacent wall. On a table in front of the couch was a vase containing yellow daffodils. The rug was the establishment's light brown shag rug. In one corner was a book case.

There was a handsome wood table against one wall with four chairs around it. Dolores had an elegant lace tablecloth on the table.

She was listening to one of Wagner's works. Richard thought it was "Tristan and Isolde".

Dolores said, "Would you like to sit on this chair and we can talk? Would you like some coffee?"

Richard sat down and said, "Yes, coffee would be fine."

She moved towards the kitchen. "Do you use milk and sugar?"

Richard answered, "A little milk, please."

Dolores turned down the volume on the record player as she passed it on her way to the kitchen.

Dolores took a few minutes to start the coffee and then looked around the corner to say, "Ralph Jenkins upstairs is also a good friend of Caspar DuBois."

Richard answered, "Yes, I know. I have him on my list."

A minute later, Dolores emerged from the kitchen with two coffees with saucers on a serving tray along with a plate of cookies on the tray.

"My, that looks great!" exclaimed Richard with a smile.

Dolores placed the tray on the table near Richard and then sat on the couch, herself.

Richard reached for his coffee and two cookies. "You have a very pleasant apartment, Dolores Jones."

"I like to keep things bright and cheerful," responded Dolores.

Richard took out his notebook and began, "I have in my notes that you spoke to Caspar DuBois in the sitting room downstairs one afternoon soon after he bought his new wrist watch."

"Yes, that's true," answered Dolores. "I was down there one afternoon and Caspar DuBois came in with his new wrist watch. He wanted to show it off a bit, I guess. He also brought his old computer with him."

"Is there Wi-Fi in this building?" asked Richard.

"Yes," answered Dolores. "That's one of the benefits of living here."

"Do people fairly often go down to the sitting room to run their computers?" asked Richard.

"Well, or to read the newspaper or watch television," answered Dolores. "I actually go down there to visit. I can run my computer up here or watch television up here by myself."

"So, you like to visit with the other tenants in the sitting room," said Richard.

"Yes," responded Dolores.

"On the day Dubois showed up with his new wrist watch, was there anyone else besides yourself there?" asked Richard.

"Typically, there are four or five of us sitting around talking," she answered. "But the day Dubois came in with his computer and new watch there was just me and Alfred Johansson. I guess it was a little early; usually there are five or six of us there around 8:00 PM. As I recall, the day Caspar DuBois walked in with his new watch, only Alfred Johansson and I were there."

"Just the two of you, at that time, then," said Richard.

"Yes," answered Dolores. "I was reading the newspaper and Alfred Johansson was sitting in the corner watching TV."

"When Dubois walked in with his computer and started talking about his new watch, did Alfred Johansson show any interest?" asked Richard.

"Not that I recall," said Dolores. "He just watched his television show."

"OK," said Richard. "So when Caspar DuBois walked in, do you recall what Dubois said?"

"Well, he said that he had just bought the watch at Emerald City Diamond on Fourth Avenue," said Dolores. "He also said he was having a little trouble running his computer. He had an old computer but he had just bought a new operating system for it and he was having trouble running his old computer with the new operating system."

"Did you help him with his computer?" asked Richard.

"Yes, I tried," answered Dolores, "but I wasn't very helpful because I wasn't familiar with Operating System 6 and that is what Caspar was having trouble with."

"Well, computers certainly can be frustrating," said Richard.

"I'll say," responded Dolores.

After a pause, she went on, "Anyway, after a little while, Ralph Jenkins walked into the sitting room. Now, Ralph Jenkins is a computer expert. He can run just about any computer it seems to me."

"Is this the Ralph Jenkins who lives on the fifth floor

of your building?" asked Richard. He had been recording Dolores' responses, and now paged through his notes to find his references to Ralph Jenkins.

"Yes, Ralph Jenkins," said Dolores. "He lives on the fifth floor of our building. Ralph Jenkins has several computers in his room I have been told. I suppose some of them use the operating system that Caspar DuBois just purchased."

"So, did he come over and help Caspar DuBois and you?" asked Richard.

"Yes," answered Dolores. "He came over and immediately took an interest in Caspar's old computer with its new operating system."

"Did Dubois tell Jenkins that he had just bought a new watch?" asked Richard.

"Yes," answered Dolores. "Caspar told him he had bought it recently at Emerald City Diamond on Fourth Avenue for $225."

"Anyway," continued Dolores, "Ralph had Caspar's computer running smoothly in just a few minutes. We had been stuck somewhere out on the Internet."

"Did Jenkins write down any helpful information on a piece of paper that Dubois could use in the future with his new operating system?" asked Richard.

"No," answered Dolores. "I think he mentioned a book Dubois could buy in a bookstore that has all kinds of useful information on Operating System 6."

"I have seen books entitled 'Operating System 6 For Dummies' on shelves in book stores," responded Richard with a smile.

"Yes," answered Dolores, laughing. "I have seen those books myself."

"Did Jenkins comment on the price that Caspar DuBois paid for his new wrist watch?" asked Richard.

"I think he said that $225 is quite a high price for a new watch," answered Dolores.

"Did anyone else walk into the room while Ralph Jenkins was helping you two?" asked Richard.

"Well, once we got Caspar's computer to run smoothly, we started talking about the traffic congestion during the previous night's Seahawk football game," answered Dolores.

"Yes, that is a problem," responded Richard.

"When we got going on that, Caspar DuBois turned off his computer," said Dolores. "Soon after that, several people walked into the sitting room and we got to talking about what the traffic would be like at the Seattle Center if we got another basketball team."

"I think the city has improved the traffic access to the Seattle Center from the freeway," said Richard.

"Well, that remains to be seen," said Dolores.

Richard folded his notebook and put it in his pocket. He said, "Thank you for the coffee and cookies, Dolores. Your information has been helpful."

Dolores and Richard stood and Richard moved towards the door.

"Do you have any suspect for the robbery yet?" asked Dolores. After a moment, she said, "I suppose you are not allowed to answer questions like that."

"It is too early for us to say anything definite on that," Richard mentioned.

Richard opened the door, smiled at Dolores, and said, "Thank you again for your information," and left.

CHAPTER 7

Richard looked at his watch and noted that it was 1:45 PM. He decided to interview Ralph Jenkins, if he was home. He looked at the list of people that Dubois had spoken to in his apartment building. The manager had said that Ralph Jenkins was in room 502. Richard took the stairs to the fifth floor.

He found room 502 and knocked on the door. There was no immediate answered so he knocked again. Richard could hear some movement inside, and presently Jenkins opened the door and looked out.

"Yes?" said Jenkins.

"I am looking for Ralph Jenkins," said Richard. "My name is Richard Hopkins. I am a Seattle police detective." He showed Jenkins his police badge.

"I am Ralph Jenkins," responded Jenkins. "What is this about?"

Richard said, "We are investigating the robbery of Caspar DuBois. I am conducting routine interviews with the friends and acquaintances of Mr. Dubois. May I come in?"

Jenkins thought a moment and then opened the door. "OK," he said.

Richard stepped into room 502. It had the same layout

as the other one-bedroom apartments. One window in Jenkin's apartment faced the alley, not Third Avenue. The walls were the standard light brown daubed plaster of the building. He had venetian blinds at the window. The rugs were the beige colored shag carpets used in the building. Ralph Jenkins did not spend a lot of time or money on decorating his apartment. He did have a large collection of computer equipment.

There was a book case against one wall. Richard glanced at the books in it and noticed that about half the books were computer manuals. There was a leather couch and matching chair. A number of magazines were scattered on the floor and some dirty plates were on the table in front of the couch. Ralph Jenkins wore light brown wash pants and a T-shirt.

"You have quite a varied assortment of computer equipment, Mr. Jenkins," said Richard.

"Yes," answered Ralph. "I spend a lot of time on my computers."

"Do you have a job, Mr. Jenkins?" asked Richard.

"I work at University Computers on Fourth Avenue," answered Jenkins.

"So, you sell computers and software," said Richard.

"Well, yes, I am a salesperson. Everyone is to some extent in that store," responded Jenkins. "However, I work mostly in the repair department there."

"I think I was in there once," said Richard. "It seemed to have an extensive collection of computer stuff."

"Yeah, this one downtown on Fourth Avenue is actually an extension of the University Computers store in the University District," said Ralph.

"Caspar DuBois mentioned that you were helping him

learn Operating System 6 that he had installed on his old computer," said Richard.

"Yes," answered Ralph. "Dubois had just bought a new Operating System 6 operating system for his old computer."

"Did you help him out, or work with him in the sitting room downstairs?" asked Richard.

"Yes," answered Ralph. "I go down to the sitting room for an hour or so a couple of times a week to look through the newspaper or watch the news on TV."

"So, you saw Richard Dubois down there one night," said Richard. "Was he talking to someone?"

"Ah, yes," answered Jenkins. "As I recall, he was talking to Dolores Jones."

"Did you speak to them?" asked Richard.

"Yes," answered Jenkins. "When I walked in Dolores saw me and said, 'Here is Ralph Jenkins, he knows all about computers'. So, I went over to find out what they were talking about."

"What was that?" asked Richard.

"Well, Caspar DuBois had recently bought a new operating system, Operating System 6, for his old computer. He was having trouble running it," said Ralph.

"So, did you join in the discussion and try to help Dubois?" asked Richard.

"Yes," answered Ralph. "We got his computer to run okay."

"Do you remember if anyone else was in the room?" asked Richard.

"Ah, I am trying to recall," said Ralph. After a moment he continued, "Johansson was in the corner watching TV. There wasn't anyone else."

"Did Dubois talk about anything else while you were there?" asked Richard.

"Dubois showed Dolores and me his brand-new wrist watch," said Ralph. "It was a beauty. Dubois said it cost $225."

"That was the watch that was stolen from Dubois," said Richard.

"How much do you think a thief could get for it at a pawnshop?" asked Ralph.

"Probably around $125," responded Richard.

"I had the impression that new watches typically sold for about $100," said Ralph.

"Do you know if Dubois showed off his new watch to other people?" asked Richard.

"I know he frequented Arnold's Broiler," said Ralph. "He might have shown it to someone there."

"So, he showed his new watch to you and Dolores Jones in the sitting room," said Richard. "Do you know if he talked to anyone else in your apartment building about his new watch?"

"Well, not that I heard of," answered Ralph. "But he might have."

"If someone stole a wrist watch and wanted to sell it, where do you suppose he would try to sell it?" asked Richard.

"I don't know," answered Ralph. "New watches are sold in jewelry shops and large department stores but I don't know if they sell secondhand watches in those places. Probably not." answered Ralph.

"Do you suppose that a thief would try to pawn it?" asked Richard.

"Pawn it," exclaimed Ralph. "I doubt he would try that.

I imagine that a person who had his new watch stolen would report it to the police department and the police would notify pawn shops to watch for it."

"Maybe you are right," said Richard.

"I suppose this thief, you are referring to, might try to sell it on the Internet. There could be an Internet store where second hand watches are sold," said Ralph.

He paused a second and then continued, "You could advertise something and then wait to be contacted."

He paused again for a minute and then continued, "Most items sold on such an Internet store are proper and legally acquired items. The same is true at swap meets."

Richard stood and said, "Well, thank you very much for your time, Ralph Jenkins. You have been most helpful."

They shook hands and Richard headed for the door.

When Richard got back to the squad room, Alister was not at his desk. Richard decided to sit down and update his computer records of the case. After about an hour he decided to quit for the day and go home. Alister had not come in yet and Richard recalled that Alister had said that they should interview their people today, Friday, and come in to the office tomorrow, Saturday, and discuss the results of the interviews.

So, Richard put his on his jacket and headed out.

The next day, Saturday, September 17, Richard left home early for the office. It was a beautiful day with the sun shining brightly. Richard arrived at the police station and parked in his assigned slot. He noticed on his watch when he entered the building that it was 8:05 am. He decided to get a coffee at the Randolph's Coffee Shop in the lobby before heading upstairs.

When Richard entered his cubicle in the squad room with his coffee, he noticed that Alister was not there yet. However, only a few minutes later Alister arrived.

Alister said, "Good morning Richard. "How are you today?"

Richard responded, "Hi, Alister. Maybe we can relax a bit today and stay in the office instead of running around town."

"Yes, we can discuss how our interviews went," said Alister. "It will be nice to sit here and relax instead of dashing around town."

They both got their notebooks out and swiveled their chairs around to face each other. "Why don't you start with your interviews at DuBois' apartment building," said Alister.

Richard stopped leafing through his notebook and began, "I spoke to David Simmons first. He lives in room 105 of their building. David Simmons is an accountant. He has gray hair and he wears eye glasses. He was dressed in blue jeans and a T-shirt when he answered the door."

Richard consulted his notes and continued, "Simmons said that Caspar DuBois had shown him and Charles Wilson his new watch. Simmons and Wilson had been standing in the hallway of their building talking about something.

DuBois happened to come along the hallway and joined their conversation. Dubois told them he had just bought the watch at Emerald City Diamond Store."

"What specifically did they talk about?" asked Alister.

"Caspar DuBois' old computer had Operating System 5. Dubois recently bought a new operating system, Operating System 6, and installed it. He was having some trouble running his computer with the new operating system, and was asking his friends for help.

DuBois knew that both David Simmons and Charles Wilson were adept in the use of computers and so DuBois asked if they would be willing to go with him to his room and help him get his computer running properly. They complied, and the three of them went to DuBois' room to work on his computer."

Richard continued, "Dubois, of course, showed David Simmons his new wrist watch. Simmons, of course, greatly admired it."

"Does David Simmons have a computer of his own?" asked Alister.

"Yes. In fact all five of the tenants I spoke to at the house had computers of their own," answered Richard.

Richard looked through his notes and said, "Other than some small talk about operating systems, nothing much was said."

Richard looked through his note book again and continued, "I next spoke to Charles Wilson. He lives in apartment 401 of DuBois' house. Charles Wilson is a young man, probably about 28 years of age. He works as a math teacher in one of the community colleges in town. He is about 5 foot 10 inches tall and is a little overweight for that height. He has a short trim mustache and wears eye glasses."

Richard turned to the next page of his notes and continued, "Wilson's story agrees pretty much with David Simmons' account. Caspar DuBois had asked Wilson and Simmons to help him with a difficulty he had encountered while running his computer. He talked mostly about operating systems. Charles Wilson said that Dubois told him that he paid $225 for his new watch."

"OK," responded Alister. "What about the third person in the sitting room, Alfred Johanssson?"

"Alfred Johansson," said Richard, looking in his notebook. "Alfred Johansson lives in room 308. Pretty much the same story as the other two. Some talk about operating systems. Alfred Johansson is familiar with Operating System 6."

Richard paged through his notes again, and continued, "Dolores Jones lives in room 406. She is a young woman about 30 years old. She wore a dress and high heels when she came to the door. She works as an accountant in a law office downtown. She uses a computer every day and so is very competent in the use of computers."

Richard continued, "Our interview proceeded pretty much along the same line as did the other three interviews."

"More talk about DuBois' computer problem?" asked Alister.

"Yes," answered Richard. "The only difference is that Dubois and Dolores were talking in the visiting room on the first floor of DuBois' building. Dubois was pretty frustrated with his computer I guess and would soon get into talking about it no matter how the conversation otherwise began."

"What did Dolores say?" asked Alister.

"Well," answered Richard, "she said she was talking with Dubois in the visiting room downstairs one day and they started talking about the weather or something. And before long, he switched the conversation to his computer problem."

"Did Dubois think that Dolores knew a lot about computers?" asked Alister.

"I suppose so," answered Richard.

"Did the conversation ever get to talk about his new wristwatch?" asked Alister.

"Dolores said that they talked about his new watch," answered Richard.

"I suppose quite a few people at that house knew about his new watch," said Alister. "He did show it around and was proud of it."

"Yes, I guess so," responded Richard. "Anyway, Dolores tried to help DuBois with his computer but wasn't very successful. However, before long, Ralph Jenkins entered the sitting room and Dolores called him over to help them with the computer."

Richard paged through his notes some and said, "Next, I spoke to Ralph Jenkins. He lives in room 502. Ralph Jenkins is a young man, probably about 25. He works as a computer programmer and repairman at University Computers on Fourth Avenue, down town. He has long hair. He was wearing light brown wash pants and a T-shirt when he answered the door. He is about 5 foot 10 inches tall and weighs the average amount for that height. He does not have a mustache or beard."

Richard continued, "He spent quite a bit of time helping Dubois with his computer. Jenkins went down to their sitting room one evening and saw Dubois and Dolores Jones there struggling with his computer."

"Did he mention how much time he spent with Dubois helping him?" asked Alister.

"I think he said it didn't take very long to straighten out DuBois' problem on that occasion," answered Richard.

"Jenkins is very knowledgeable about computers," said Richard, "and was able to help Dubois through a lot of his troubles."

"It seems that Dubois' computer would just get stuck or stalled out on the Internet fairly often," continued Richard. "Dubois didn't know what led up to the situation, and so he didn't know how to avoid it," said Richard.

"Did Jenkins know?" asked Alister.

"I guess so," answered Richard. "I think he told Dubois to slow down and give the computer time to download stuff from the Internet before entering a new command – or something like that. I am not sure exactly what he told Dubois. It seemed kind of vague to me."

"Well did Jenkins seem to resolve the problem that Dubois had?" asked Alister.

"Yes, he did," answered Richard.

"So Jenkins is very knowledgeable about computers," remarked Alister. "You did say that he is a computer programmer didn't you? Is that his job?"

"Yes, he told me that he works as a programmer or computer repair man at University Computers downtown," answered Richard. "Maybe he's just interested in computers and spends a lot of his spare time running computers."

"Yeah," I know there are people like that," remarked Alister.

"I am glad Jenkins could help Dubois," said Richard. "But that doesn't help us much to advance our case."

"No, it doesn't," said Alister. "We're looking for an instance or occasion where someone showed a great interest in Dubois' ring or his watch, or how much he paid for it. But we are not hearing of such an occasion."

"Right," responded Richard.

"Did any of the people you interviewed recall anyone showing a great interest in Dubois' ring?" asked Alister.

"No," answered Richard. "Nobody commented on his ring."

"So, they spent their time helping Caspar DuBois become acquainted with Operating System 6," said Alister. "There wasn't much beyond that?" asked Alister.

"No. That was all I got," answered Richard.

CHAPTER 8

Alister then went on to describe his investigation. He began, "I went to the Fourth Avenue and Pine Street 24 hour clinic where Caspar DuBois was treated. I spoke to the nurse who treated him. I managed to get some bandages he was wearing. They hadn't thrown the garbage out yet. I took the bandages over to the lab to test for DNA. Caspar DuBois got into a fight with his assailant and maybe his assailant's blood was on the bandages as well as Caspar DuBois' blood. I gave the bandages to Ralph Lee at the crime lab on Rainier Avenue and told him we would get a sample of Dubois' blood to him in a day or two."

"We have a sample of Dubois' blood now," said Richard. "When he showed up at the police station to file his case after talking to us Thursday morning, they noticed his bandages and they sent him to the hospital to have one of the doctors check him."

"OK," said Alister. "We want to get a sample of his blood to Ralph Lee at the DNA lab."

Alister continued, "I then went to see the three women Caspar DuBois knows from Arnold's Broiler. We might have a lead here."

Alister got out his notebook and related his conversations

with Charlene Heath, Jennifer Worthington, and Janet Smith. When Alister finished, he said, "This man, Siegfried Stone, is a person of interest."

"Yes. I think you're right," said Richard. "He showed an interest in the wrist watch as well as the old computer."

"Right," said Alister. "He spoke to Caspar DuBois about his watch on more than one occasion. He even asked Dubois how much the watch cost on one occasion."

Richard said, "And, he went over to the table at Arnold's Broiler where Dubois and the ladies were talking about the computer."

"Of course, just showing an interest in a watch that an acquaintance just purchased doesn't mean anything. All the other people we interviewed spoke to Caspar DuBois about his new watch," said Alister.

"Right. They all knew him and showed an interest in his new toy," said Richard.

"Still, I think we will speak to Siegfried Stone," said Alister.

"I'll see if I can get his address from the Motor Vehicle Department," said Richard turning to his computer.

Alister sat down at his computer and entered into the Caspar DuBois case all the information he had gathered from his interviews the previous day. He then filled out the form that requests the doctor at the hospital to send a sample of Caspar DuBois' blood to the DNA lab for testing.

Alister said, "I might need a Probable Cause document from a judge at court to get the doctor or hospital to send a blood sample of Caspar DuBois to our DNA lab for testing."

Monday morning, Alister took his Probable Cause document to Judge Jones' chambers in the courthouse to get it signed. He explained to the judge that the presence of blood and DNA from someone other than Caspar DuBois on Caspar DuBois' bandage could lead to the person who attacked him. The judge signed the document and Alister took it to the hospital to get the hospital to send a blood sample of Caspar DuBois to Ralph Lee at the DNA lab.

When Alister got to the police detective office it was 10:30 AM. Richard Hopkins was at his desk and said, "I have the address where Siegfried Stone lives plus a few other things. Siegfried Stone was convicted of theft in Portland in 2005 and spent one year at Wilson jail."

"Let's go have a conversation with Mr. Stone," said Alister.

They took the stairs down to the police garage and signed out an unmarked police car. They drove up to 1608 First Avenue.

"He lives in room 205 at this address," said Richard. They parked in a no parking zone and put a Seattle police card on the dashboard.

They went up to room 205 and knocked. Siegfried Stone opened the door and said, "Yes?"

Alister showed Siegfried his police badge and said, "We are investigating the robbery of Caspar DuBois and heard that you are an acquaintance of his. We are conducting routine questioning of all of Mr. Dubois' friends and acquaintances. May we come in?"

Siegfried Stone opened the door and gestured them in. Stone lived in an apartment similar to that of Caspar DuBois. It was a single room. There was a door in one wall leading into a bathroom. The apartment had a Murphy bed along one wall. It consisted of a fancy glass paneled door with a curtain behind the glass. If you opened the door there was the bed mounted on a vertical pole. If one turned the bed on its pole, it was possible to lower the bed onto the floor in the living room. Immediately behind the pole was a small dresser and some closet space.

All in all, the apartment was kind of dark and dingy. There was a large window on the wall to the left, but the drapes were drawn across it.

"Is there any kind of view from this building?" asked Richard.

"Not really," answered Siegfried Stone, laughing. "If you open those drapes you will see a brick building across the alley from here. Another apartment building with windows like these."

Stone looked kind of scruffy himself. He hadn't shaved that morning. Perhaps he had taken a shower. Siegfried Stone had long unkempt hair, although it wasn't long enough to reach to his shoulders. It was a medium brown in color. He was cultivating a beard. It was not the thick bushy variety; it was of medium length. He had a full mustache. He was just under six feet in height and was quite thin. He might have just gotten up within the last hour and taken a shower. He was wearing a white T-shirt and blue jeans with frayed cuffs. He didn't have shoes or socks on. Stone had a brown jacket hanging on a hook near the door. No umbrella was in sight.

Stone motioned the detectives to a couple of chairs and they all sat down. Stone tried to be affable and said, "Can I offer you gentlemen some coffee? I made it not too long ago." He looked at his watch and said, "Actually, an hour ago."

Alister smiled and answered, "Thank you. That would be fine."

Siegfried rose and moved toward the kitchen alcove in one corner of the apartment. "Milk, sugar?" he asked.

Alister answered, "I'll take it black, thank you."

Richard responded, "Milk for me, please. No sugar."

Alister and Richard looked around the room. The walls were done in a rough daubed plaster form, painted beige. Curtains were at the one window, which looked out on another building. The rugs had a dark geometric pattern. The furniture consisted of a couch with two matching chairs, a table, two easy chairs, and a book case containing a few books and several decorative statutes or figurines.

Siegfried stepped forward with the coffee cups on a tray. "I hope it is hot enough," he said. When Siegfried finished serving, he sat at the table and asked, "Well, what would you like to know?"

Alister took out his notebook and pencil and said, "This is just a routine investigation, Mr. Stone. We have to interview everyone who knows Caspar DuBois or is a friend of his."

Siegfried nodded. He said, "Yes, certainly. I understand."

Alister began, "Mr. Stone, are you employed at present?"

Siegfried responded, "I work part time as a cook at a hamburger restaurant on Sixth Avenue."

"Is that where you cut your hand? I noticed a bandage on your left hand," asked Alister.

"No," returned Siegfried. "I actually cut my finger over at Caspar DuBois' apartment last Tuesday. I accidentally dropped the glass of wine that Caspar poured for me. I cut my finger on the broken glass when I bent down to pick up the pieces."

"Did it bleed much?" asked Alister.

"Not too much," answered Siegfried. "I went into the bathroom to put a band aid on it. Caspar was very solicitous and gave me a bandage. I guess I bled a drop or two in the living room and a drop or two in the bathroom."

"Do you visit with Caspar DuBois very often?" asked Alister.

"I don't visit with him at his apartment very often," answered Siegfried. "I do see him at Arnold's Broiler fairly often."

"He recently bought a new watch," said Alister. "I think he said that he showed it to you at Arnold's Broiler."

"Yes, he did," responded Siegfried. "He was in Arnold's Broiler working with a new operating system he had installed on his old computer and was having some trouble. We were helping him with that."

"Do you have a computer, Mr. Stone?" asked Alister.

"Yes, I do," answered Stone. "It is kind of old fashion by today's standards, I guess. I bought it secondhand years ago. It's a table top computer. Not the kind you walk around with."

Richard asked, "Can you get up on the Internet with it?"

"Oh, yes, of course," answered Stone. "You just need an Ethernet connection. I got that with my cable company's TV and phone connection."

"So, you can get up on the Internet," said Alister.

"Well yes, certainly," answered Stone, "but my old computer is very slow and surfing the Internet is very frustrating."

"You can buy a new computer these days for $300," said Richard. "That should overcome some of your frustration."

"No doubt you are right," said Stone. "But I seldom use

my computer for anything. I send emails to my friends, but that's about all."

Alister leafed through his notes a bit. "I think Janet Smith said you and she were helping Caspar DuBois with his new operating system over at Arnold's Broiler one day."

"Yes," answered Siegfried Stone. "Janet was fairly adept at Operating System 6."

"I noticed that you have quite a few statutes or figurines in your book case," said Alister, gesturing towards the bookcase. "Did you acquire these in Seattle shops?"

"Some of these I found in the pawn shops on First Avenue. The rest I buy from a friend of mine who frequents the secondhand outdoor swap meets in California," answered Siegfried.

"Is this a person who is a resident of Seattle and who travels down to California to attend swap meets?" asked Alister.

"Yes," answered Stone. "He lives on Denny Street."

"Could you tell us his name?" asked Richard.

"His name is Edward Atinsky," answered Stone.

"Are you saying Edward Atinsky buys secondhand items in pawn shops and garage sales and then he goes down to California to sell them at swap meets at a slight markup?" asked Richard.

"That's right," answered Stone. "Then he buys secondhand things at the swap meet and brings them up here to sell them at a slight markup."

"And you have bought some of the vases and statues in this room from him. Is that correct?" asked Alister.

"Yes, that is correct," answered Stone.

Alister put his cup down and said, "Thank you for the

coffee. I guess we don't have any more questions at this time. I wonder if I could use your bathroom before I leave?"

"Yes, sure," answered Siegfried. "It is over there," pointing at the bathroom door.

Alister and Richard got up and Alister moved toward the bathroom. Siegfried asked Richard how Caspar's wounds were healing.

Alister entered the bathroom and closed the door. He flushed the toilet and turned on the water faucet. He made a quick search of the bathroom. Under the sink in a pail, he found a black ski mask. A quick examination of it revealed a cut or tear near the left ear. Alister put the mask back exactly as he found it.

Alister opened the door of a small closet in the bathroom. There were boxes of soap on a shelf and bottles of bleach. Alister didn't see a washing machine or drier. He assumed that there was one or more laundry rooms in the apartment building that the tenants could use. Such facilities required a lot of quarters.

Alister lifted things on the floor and shelves and peered under them to check for hidden items. There was a cloth bag on the floor near the back of the closet. Alister picked it up and looked inside. It contained some tools. There was a hammer, several screwdrivers, a couple of chisels, and a crowbar. There was also a roll of masking tape. Alister thought such a tool kit could be used for breaking and entering. Alister didn't have any more time and therefore he left the bathroom.

When he emerged from the bathroom, Richard and Siegfried were still talking about Caspar's wounds and his trip to the Pine Street 24 hour clinic.

CHAPTER 9

When Alister and Richard were back in the police car they began talking about their interview with Siegfried Stone.

Alister said, "His cut finger might just be a precautionary measure he took a couple days before his planned robbery."

"Right," responded Richard. "He figured if a fight ensued during the robbery he might get cut and bleed a little in the apartment. Thus, we will have his blood and be able to get his DNA."

"Yes," continued Alister. "He will be able to say that the reason his blood is there is because he cut his finger on the broken coffee cup a couple days before the robbery. Not because he was there at the time of the robbery."

"Yes, it is just careful preparation for a crime," said Richard. "We won't be able to prove anything from the DNA."

"Of course, we might be able to argue in the courtroom about where the DNA was found," said Alister.

"The DNA from the coffee cup will be found in the living room and bathroom," said Richard. "Whereas, the DNA on Caspar DuBois' bandages was found on the bandages."

"I'll checked with Ralph Lee at the crime lab this

afternoon," said Alister. "Maybe the hospital got Caspar DuBois' blood sample to him. I doubt it, though, since I just sent the judge's order to the hospital recently.

Alister continued, "While I was in the bathroom at Siegfried Stone's apartment, I hunted around a bit. I found a ski mask in a pail under the sink. It was black and was torn near the left ear. It would be hard to use that information for anything unless we could find some of Caspar DuBois' DNA on it."

"He might have washed it off," put in Richard.

"I don't think we could get the search warrant to retrieve the ski mask," said Alister. "A probable cause argument would be a little too weak."

"What about the friend who goes to swap meets in California?" asked Richard.

"The person who supposedly sells him the statues on his book case?" asked Alister.

"It would be pretty hard to identify or locate him, I suppose," responded Richard.

"He might have taken the wrist watch or ring to California," said Alister. "We will have to interview the people at Arnold's Broiler again and ask about Siegfried Stone's acquaintances."

After a pause, Alister went on, "I think Siegfried Stone needs money quite badly. He might not be able to wait several weeks for a stolen article to go all the way down to some California swap meet to get sold. It might take several days for it to get sold and then Siegfried's friend has to bring the money back here."

"Do you think he sold it to a pawnshop here?" asked Richard.

"Probably," said Alister. "We will have to check pawn shops up here on the North end and some others on the South end."

"We have Siegfried's photograph," said Richard.

"I think we will have to divide up the pawn shops between us and start conducting interviews soon, maybe Wednesday," said Alister.

After lunch, Alister headed down to the police crime lab on Rainier Avenue.

The lab was in a renovated machine shop on Rainier Avenue. It had been a four story brick building with ample window space. The city had acquired it ten years ago. It was a good sturdy building since it was built to house heavy machinery on several floors. The police department had purchased a lot of lab equipment and installed it in the building. Approximately two hundred people reported to work at the lab every day.

Alister parked in the parking lot in the rear and enter the rear door. Holding his badge to the badge reader and putting his right hand on the electronic hand and fingerprint reader got him into the building.

Alister took the elevator up to the fourth floor and went to Ralph Lee's office. He notice that the door was ajar. Alister knocked but heard nothing. He opened the door slightly and glanced in. Ralph wasn't there. However, since his door was ajar, Alister figured he hadn't left the building and was probably in one of the labs. So, Alister went down to the labs on the third floor and started down the hall, looking in the labs as he proceeded.

When he came to the DNA and fingerprint lab, he thought he would find him there. However, Lee wasn't there so Alister continued down the hall and finally found Lee in the cloth and fabric lab talking to Monica Jackson.

Alister knocked on the door and entered. When Ralph Lee and Monica looked over, Alister said, "Hi, Ralph. I thought I would stop over and see if the hospital had sent over Caspar DuBois' blood sample yet."

"Hello, Alister," said Ralph Lee. "Monica, this is Alister Jensen, a Seattle police department detective."

Monica and Alister exchange greetings.

Ralph went on, "Monica and I were just discussing the results of the lab examination of the fabric from the trunk of an abandoned car found in West Seattle last Thursday."

"Did you come up with anything useful?" asked Alister.

"Maybe," answered Monica.

Ralph said, "We did receive Caspar DuBois' blood sample from the hospital."

"Let's go to my office," said Ralph, motioning towards the door. So long, Monica, I'll speak to you later."

They proceeded to Ralph's office. Alister sat down in the chair near Ralph's desk while Ralph went to a cabinet to get a folder.

When Ralph was seated at his desk, he opened the folder and said, "We have some DNA analyzing equipment here, but we also send samples to the state lab in Olympia and also to the FBI lab in Washington."

Ralph took several fairly long graphs from the envelope and laid them on the desk for Alister to see.

Ralph continued, "We sent all of the bandages in that bag you brought from the Pine Street Clinic as well as Caspar DuBois' blood sample from the hospital to one of the labs we use. They compared the bandages with Caspar DuBois' blood sample and were able to decide which bandages had been on Caspar DuBois. They then ran an electropherogram on Dubois' bandages."

He gestured at the graphs on his desk, "Here is a copy of some of them."

Alister looked at the graphs more closely.

"You can see," continued Ralph, "that the graph is basically a horizontal line with several groups of peaks located on the horizontal line every inch or so. You can see that one group of peaks has the color green, while the next group has the color blue, while the following group of peaks has the color yellow. Each group of peaks represents a locus on the chromosome. This DNA machine examines 14 loci."

Ralph reached into his desk drawer and took out a pencil to point with. "Notice," he said, "that in every group of vertical peaks, a few peaks are of one height while a few other peaks are of a higher or greater height. This usually means that there is more than one person's blood in the sample."

Ralph looked at Alister to see if he was acknowledging or appreciating this important point.

"So, you think we might have both the victim's blood sample and the perpetrator's blood sample," said Alister.

"Exactly," responded Ralph.

"We do have a possible suspect," went on Alister, "but, we don't have a blood sample from him yet."

Ralph said, "Well, we were able to extract a blood smear with DNA of the second person from the bandage. We send it to the FBI in Washington. They have a database of DNA profiles from crime scenes across the country called CODIS. We haven't heard back yet."

Alister rose and said, "Thank you for your time, Ralph. I'll come back in a day or two."

Alister headed back to the police station. He wanted to go to his office and use his computer to enter all the information he had gleaned on the case over the past couple of days. The police files and records have to be kept up to date and complete. When he got to the office, Richard was sitting there at his own computer.

Alister said, "I was just over at the lab. The hospital complied with the judge's order and sent a sample of Caspar DuBois' blood over to the police lab."

"Well, that was fast," said Richard. "Did the lab discover anything?"

"They were able to use the hospital's blood sample to decide which of the Fourth and Pine clinic's bandages came from Caspar DuBois," answered Alister.

"That's good," said Richard.

"The lab uses a kind of graph called an electropherogram to analyze blood samples. The graph indicates that there were blood samples with DNA from two different people on Caspar DuBois' bandages."

"Right," said Richard. "The victim and the attacker."

"Ralph Lee sent a sample of the attacker's blood to the FBI in Washington. They are going to see if the attacker is in their CODIS database," continued Alister.

"Maybe they will find that it is Siegfried Stone's blood. Remember, he was arrested several times already," said Richard.

"Yes," responded Alister, "but remember Stone was at Richard Dubois' apartment a day or so before the robbery and manage to cut his finger on a broken glass cup."

"Clever man," said Richard. "His lawyer will point out to the jury that Siegfried's blood and DNA on Caspar DuBois' bandage came from that accident in Dubois' apartment."

"I think tomorrow I'll go to Forensics and check on things," said Alister. You should probably go to Arnold's Broiler and try to get a lead on the California swap meet acquaintance."

Alister put in an hour on his computer updating the record of the robbery. Then he headed home.

Alister had a condo on Capitol Hill. It was on Summit Avenue facing west. As he drove up Denny Avenue before he turned onto Summit, he noticed again the relatively unattractive looking businesses along the street. He thought that a main street like Denny Avenue at that close proximity to downtown would have a lot of flashy up-to-date business establishments. But instead, some of them looked almost like garages or storage buildings.

When he got home, he parked in his garage space and walked up the two flights of stairs to his condo. He turned on the lights and took his shoes off, leaving them on the mat by the door. He opened the blinds over the door leading out onto the balcony and opened the door. It was still warm out and the air smelled clean.

He headed to the kitchen to start a pot of coffee. He opened the refrigerator and took out a raspberry muffin on a plate. When the coffee was ready, he poured a cup and went with the muffin and coffee out onto his balcony. The sun was setting in the West. Since it had been a relatively clear day, the sun setting and the Olympic Mountains were clearly visible. And of course, the space needle was visible since it is close enough to be visible in clear weather or overcast weather. Alister was glad that they had taken down that second restaurant - or whatever it was - halfway up the Space Needle Tower.

Alister's thoughts turned to the robbery case. What good would it do if they could prove that the other blood and DNA on Caspar DuBois' bandage belong to Siegfried Stone. Any effective lawyer could tell the jury that Siegfried had cut his finger and bled a little in Caspar DuBois' living room a day or two before the robbery.

Alister ruminated again on the topic of DNA. Sometimes, DNA can be contaminated by the police if the samples get a little water on them or are left in the sun light too long. But the big thing is that even if the DNA is valid, there might be more than one way to explain how it got on the crime scene. DNA is easily one of the most reliable pieces of evidence but it can get on the crime scene for several different reasons. One way is that the suspect left the DNA during the crime. Another, is that the suspect just visited the victim and scene just days earlier. Another is that somebody planted the DNA on the crime scene to incriminate the suspect.

Another nagging thought was what if they had settled on a suspect too soon with too little evidence to support their choice? Maybe they should re-examine the evidence in an open minded way. For one thing, he hadn't contacted the forensic team that arrive at Caspar DuBois' apartment just before he and Richard left. Alister decided to contact them first thing in the morning.

After an hour of this kind of thinking, Alister turned to one of his favorite pastime, reading. He went to his book case and picked up his current mystery book. Alister didn't agree very much with the novelist's depiction of police methods. But, he did enjoy the author's psychological treatment of the main characters. Two of his favorite authors were Michael Connelly and Elmore Leonard. His current novel was one by Connelly. Connelly had great style; this was due to by his having been a newspaper reporter for perhaps years before becoming a mystery writer.

At 9:00 AM the next morning, Tuesday, Alister entered the north wing of the fifth floor of the police station. This is where the forensics department had its office. The space that forensics had on the fifth floor in this wing was extensive. When Alister entered the area he saw seven or eight people dressed in white coats moving about between the tables in the room and the machinery and electronic equipment along the walls. He knew that there was fingerprint analyzing equipment in here. Alister had been told that they can run a preliminary DNA sampling test in this room. A detailed analysis of DNA had to be conducted in special laboratories in the country and could take days to complete.

Alister noticed that at the far end of the wing there was the water tank into which they could fire guns found at the crime scene. They would then examine the spent bullet at the bottom of the water tank under a microscope to determine the markings caused by the barrel of the gun. In this way they could determine if the bullets found at the crime scene or remove from the victim at the hospital had been fired by the gun that was in the possession of the police. Some of the tables in the room were used to conduct chemical analyses of debris found at the crime scene. Alister knew that there were additional and more complete laboratories in the state to analyze data procured at the crime scene.

CHAPTER 10

Alister went to James Newton's office. James and his team were the people who showed up at Caspar DuBois' apartment when Richard and he were talking to Dubois. Newton was in his office so Alister knocked.

"Hi, Alister," said Newton. "Come on in."

Newton was dressed in a business suit. He wore a light brown singled breasted jacket with matching pants and a vest. He had on a light blue striped shirt and red tie. He had a trim mustache and wavy brown hair. He wore glasses. Alister knew that Newton had several degrees in chemistry and all of his assistants were highly trained.

Alister entered the office and sat in the chair that Newton motioned him to.

"Have you finished with Caspar DuBois, yet?" asked Alister. "Richard and I have been interviewing a number of the people that Caspar DuBois spoke to prior to the robbery."

"Yes, we have finished and filed our report," said Newton, rising from his desk and heading toward a file cabinet. He brought out a file and handed it to Alister.

"There was considerable evidence of a fight in the room," said Newton. Numerous things were lying on the floor, probably from a tipped over table near an easy chair. A number of items were on the floor near the bureau. Apparently, the thief was going through the bureau and placing them on the floor.

It appears that Dubois was awakened at one point and stood up to confront the invader. The sprawl of the bedsheets and blanket attest to that. The struggle moved around the room, and it appears that the intruder picked up a book end and struck Dubois. Some of Dubois' blood is on the bookend. The intruder, of course, wore gloves."

"What was the mode of entry?" asked Alister.

"The window frame was forced. It was forced, not struck. That kept the entry quiet," answered Newton. "One would think that the robber would break and enter when Dubois wasn't there."

"Maybe the robber was after something that Dubois usually carried with him," answered Alister. "So, he had to enter after Dubois returned home and went to bed."

"I suppose so," said Newton.

"We are thinking," said Alister, "that the robber entered the room quietly when Dubois was sleeping and quietly moved about taking what he wanted."

"So, you think he accidentally knocked something over and the noise awoke Dubois?" asked Newton.

"Yes," answered Alister. "Then the fight began."

"Well, the evidence does support such a scenario," remarked Newton. "The scattered debris developed after the fight began."

"Did you find any cloth or fabric to indicate what the intruder wore?" asked Alister.

"Yes, we found a number of strands of a black jacket or

parka worn by hikers and a torn piece of a pocket from a black pair of pants," said Newton.

"Did they looked like new material or pieces from old garments?" asked Alister.

"New material, for sure," answered Newton. "In fact we went over to the REI store on Denny Avenue and were able to get some samples from their hiking or camping department."

"How did you manage that?" asked Alister.

"We told the manager over there that a crime had recently occurred and we were from the police forensics team that was examining evidence from the scene."

"Did you find a pants and jacket that was made from material that resembled the pieces of cloth you found at Dubois as room?" asked Alister.

"Yes, we did," answered Newton. "The REI store manager got one of his tailors to snip a small piece or fragment off the pocket of a pair of black pants we found at the store. And, the tailor was able to snip a small piece off the inner lining of a jacket we found on one of the coat racks at the store."

"I suppose you ran a comparison of these fragments from the REI store and the evidence from Dubois' apartment," said Alister.

"You bet," answered Newton. "We sent the material to the lab and got an exact match."

"I will go over to the REI store with our suspects photograph and see if any clerk can recognize him," said Alister.

"Did you find any blood from the fight or any finger prints?" asked Alister.

"We found five or six blood drops but no fingerprints," answered Newton. "We sent the blood drops to the lab of course," said Newton.

"OK," answered Alister. "We'll check on it."

"We are pretty sure the intruder wore gloves," said Newton, "because there are no fingerprints on the window sill in Dubois' apartment where the intruder entered, and no fingerprints on the bookend that was used to strike Dubois. There are plenty of fingerprints around the apartment, but that's normal."

Alister said, "Dubois mentioned that when he woke up and finally got to his feet, he got into a fight with the intruder. Dubois said that he landed at least one good blow on the side of his assailant's jaw and knocked him down. This was before the intruder picked up the book end and struck Dubois. Thus, the intruder might have some of his own blood on his person as well as some of Dubois' blood."

"So, are you saying that the scraps of cloth we found on the floor that were torn from the intruder's clothing might have the intruder's blood as well as DuBois' blood on it?" asked Newton.

"Yes," answered Alister.

"Do you have a suspect, yet?" asked Newton.

"We have settled on a suspect," said Alister, "but we want to check all possibilities. It is possible to select the wrong suspect."

"Of course," responded Newton. "All we've got are the blood drops that were sent to the lab. We do have two fingerprints that might constitute incriminating evidence, and this will amaze you."

"Great," responded Alister. "What is that?"

"As I said," Newton responded, "we are pretty sure the intruder wore surgical-gloves. However, we think he ripped his gloves on the way down the outdoor fire escape."

"You mean thc fire escape outside Dubois' window that he used to enter and leave Dubois' apartment?" asked Alister.

"Yes," continued Newton. "The intruder had knocked Dubois unconscious with the bookend so he had a few minutes to go down the fire escape and run away. However, he would be in a hurry and under pressure."

Newton paused, and paged through the notes he had on his desk. He went on, "The intruder must have torn one of his surgical gloves on the rough iron fire escape. We found two fingerprints with blood on them on the fire escape metal surface. It's a place where the fire escape is attached to the wall of the building. It is a fairly intricate bracket consisting of several pieces of metal with bolts attached."

Alister interrupted, "Does it look like he tried to wipe off any possible fingerprints on the bracket?"

"Yes," answered Newton. "The area is smeared a bit as if the intruder figured he might have left a fingerprint and tried to wipe it off."

"He noticed that he had torn his glove and might have left a fingerprint and tried to wipe it off," said Alister. "However, he didn't have much time. Dubois might regain consciousness and yell out."

"Right," said Newton. "So, he tries to wipe away any possible fingerprints. That's what the smearing indicates. The metal bracket on the building is fairly intricate so he was only partially successful."

"I think we have something really valuable here," said Alister, smiling. "It might be possible for our suspect to explain his blood drops in Dubois' apartment. He visited Dubois a day before the robbery and conveniently cut his finger on a broken piece of glass. This put his blood in Dubois' apartment and he could therefore use this finger cutting accident to explain the presence of his blood in Dubois' apartment. He knew that Dubois might wake during the robbery and a fight ensue."

"Yeah, the bloody fingerprint on the outside fire escape really clinches it," said Newton.

"I can't imagine what the suspect's defense attorney could say to the jury to explain away his client's bloody fingerprints on the fire escape outside," said Alister.

Newton and Alister had a laugh over that.

"So you sent the bloody fingerprints from the fire escape to the crime lab along with the other fingerprints?" asked Alister.

"I sent it in a separate envelope and I included a note in the envelope stating that the fingerprint was taken from the outside fire escape," answered Newton. "I also included photographs of the fire escape bracket in my report."

"All right," said Alister, standing, "we will wait for the evidence to come back from the blood analysis and fingerprint lab. In the meantime we can check the pawn shops to see if anyone tried to hock items from Dubois' room. Is this report mine?" he asked, indicating the sheaf of papers that Newton had handed him earlier.

"Yes, you can take it," said Newton. "Everything is on the police computer system. But, I printed that for you."

"OK, thanks," said Alister. He turned and left the office.

Alister left James Newton's office and decided he would canvas the neighborhood to find out if anyone saw a person enter or leave the alley at the time of the robbery. When Richard and Alister originally responded to the police telephone call it was about 7:00 AM. After inspecting the crime scene, Alister and Richard had gone down to the alley outside Dubois' apartment to look for any evidence that the culprit might have dropped. He noticed at that time that there was a bank across the street.

He decided now to go to the bank and check if they had an outdoor camera that might have recorded a person going up and down the fire escape. Alister entered West Coast Bank and proceeded to an office where he saw a banker sitting.

Alister said, "Good afternoon. I would like some information."

The banker said, "Come in. Please sit down."

Alister entered the office and sat down. He showed the banker his badge and said, "I am a Seattle police detective investigating a robbery that occur in this neighborhood a few days ago."

The banker looked carefully at his badge and said, "My name is Jeffrey Jones. How can I help you?"

Alister said, "I noticed that you have a camera outside on the street. I suppose if records the people who use your outdoor banking equipment. I wonder if it might have recorded our suspect."

Jeffrey asked, "What was the day and time of the incident."

Alister answered, "September 15 at about 1:00 AM."

Jeffrey thought for a moment and then said, "We should have that time period still on record. We periodically erase our files. I will call someone who can run the camera for you."

He dialed a phone number and asked for Denise to come to his office. When she arrived, Jeffrey said, "Denise, this Seattle police detective, Alister Jensen, would like to see our outdoor camera coverage for September 15 at around 1:00 AM."

Jeffrey handed Alister a form and said, "Would you please fill out this form, detective."

Alister filled out the form and then Denise and Alister went down the hall to a small room where there was a lot of electronic recording equipment.

Denise said, "Please have a seat here, detective Alister Jensen, while I dial up the time period you are interested in."

Alister sat in the chair she indicated while Denise operated the equipment. Finally she stopped and said, "Here is the scene. There are two cameras. One shows the entire scene on both sides of the street, and the other camera just shows the man in front of our teller machine. The time is displayed at the top of the screen. You can advance that time sequence by clicking on this arrow at the bottom of that screen."

"Thank you, Denise," said Alister.

Alister operated the controls. The camera that depicted the entire street scene showed several people entering or leaving the alley during the relevant time period, but they were so far away and it was so dark, that it would be difficult to use the camera scene as evidence in a court room.

Alister said, "The scene is not entirely clear. However, I would like a copy of this data between 1:00 AM and 1:30 AM, please."

Denise said, "All right, I will have it in a few minutes."

She left the room and returned with a package in about 10 minutes. Alister thanked her for the package and left.

When Alister returned to his cubicle at the police station, Richard was on his computer.

"Hi," said Alister as he entered the cubicle.

"Hello," returned Richard, turning to greet him.

"We could go down to the cafeteria for lunch," said Alister, "and review our progress."

"OK," answered Richard. He got up from his desk and they headed for the elevator.

The cafeteria wasn't too crowded, yet.

"We are here a little early," said Richard. "It's only 11:15 AM," he said, glancing at his watch.

They got in the line at the cafeteria. "It looks like it's either fish, sole I guess, or lasagna," said Richard as they made their way down the line.

Alister chose lasagna, garlic bread, and coffee. Richard chose the fish. They headed for a table in the far corner where they could talk with some privacy. Nobody was in the adjacent booth and John Allen, from homicide, was at the nearest table some twenty feet away.

"We can talk a little here," said Alister, sitting down. "We'll have to go upstairs to our cubicle when it starts getting crowded."

They both sat down.

"The lasagna looks good," said Richard, "but I read recently that we don't eat enough fish."

"Fish are great," returned Alister, "provided there are adequate laws to keep industrial waste from being dumped into the bays and rivers emptying into the ocean."

Alister tasted his lasagna. "The cook did a pretty good job on the lasagna," he said.

"How are the interviews going, to change the subject?" Alister asked.

"Pretty good," said Richard. "I can give you the details when we get back to our cubicle. I left my notebook in my jacket. I have spoken to the people at Dubois' apartment building. Let's see, that's David Simmons, Charles Wilson, Dolores Jones, and Ralph Jenkins. I also spoke to the clerk at Emerald City Diamond store that sold the new watch to Dubois. He paid $225 for the watch."

At that moment, two policemen that Alister recognized from traffic enforcement sat down in the adjacent booth.

"We might as well go upstairs," said Alister. "It is starting to fill up in here."

When they got to their cubicle, Richard took his notebook from his jacket and sat down. He leafed through it for a minute, and said, "Here we are. My notes from my interview with the people in Dubois' house. I interviewed David Simmons first. He lives in room 105. He said that Caspar DuBois past him and Charles Wilson one afternoon in the hallway of their apartment building. He couldn't recall the exact date. Dubois said he had just bought a new watch, which he proudly showed them. He told Simmons and Wilson that he had also recently bought a new operating system for his old computer but was having trouble with the new operating system. He asked them if they would go to his room and help him out with his new operating system."

"This must have been Wednesday, September 7. We have to make the timeline. We might as well do it today," said Alister. "Finish with your interviews, there, and then we'll construct our timeline."

Richard resumed, "So David Simmons and Charles Wilson went with Dubois to his room. In my interview with Simmons, he said Dubois had his old computer with its new operating system on a table in his room."

"Do they have a Wi-Fi there?" asked Alister.

"I asked Simmons," said Richard, "and he said they do. Maybe, they work the Wi-Fi fee into the rent at that place."

"So, anyway," said Alister, "they got the computer to start working. What then?"

"Did Simmons say anything that would suggest that he was interested in Dubois' new watch?"

"No, nothing," answered Richard. "Simmons just described how he and Charles Wilson went to Dubois' room and helped him with his computer for a while."

"OK," said Alister. "What about your interview with Charles Wilson?"

Richard leafed through his notebook and stopped. "I interviewed Charles Wilson after talking with Simmons. Charles Wilson lives in room 401. Charles Wilson's story agrees with that of Simmons. Just the three of them running Dubois' old computer with its new operating system. Nothing else. Charles Wilson said that he told Dubois and Simmons that he had seen a new watch at a store on Third Avenue and the price was $100."

CHAPTER 11

"OK," said Alister. "So, I guess we don't get anything from David Simmons or Charles Wilson." What about the people that Dubois showed his new watch to in their sitting room?"

"That would be Dolores Jones and Ralph Jenkins," said Richard paging through his notebook. "I guess what we have to keep in mind," said Richard, "is that a new watch is not a coveted and expensive thing. A lot of these people have new watches."

Richard stopped paging and said, "Here are my notes from my interview with Dolores Jones. She lives in apartment 406. Dolores said that quite a few people in the building go down to the sitting room on the first floor to visit. She said there are typically five or six people in the sitting room almost every night at 8:00 PM. Dolores said that one particular night Dubois came down with his new watch. Dubois also had with him his old computer with its new operating system installed. Dubois could not run it very well and was frustrated. Dolores said she could not help him very much because she also had experience only with Operating System 5."

Alister asked, "Did she say who was in the sitting room that day?"

Richard looked at his notes. "I asked that and Dolores said that Alfred Johansson was in the corner watching TV."

Richard looked at his notes and went on, "Dolores said Ralph Jenkins came down a little later. She said he knew a lot about computers and took an interest in Dubois' problem. Dolores said Ralph Jenkins had Dubois' problem fixed fairly soon and then they spent almost an hour surfing around on the Internet and trying this and that."

"Did you get anything else that was helpful from Dolores?" asked Alister.

"No. Not really," said Richard.

"OK," said Alister. "Let's go on to Ralph Jenkins."

Richard returned to his notebook and turned a few pages. "I spoke to Ralph Jenkins on the same day, September 16. He is in room 502. Ralph Jenkins has a lot of computer equipment in his room. I asked him if he thought that Dubois had paid a typical or an exorbitant price for his new watch. Jenkins said that he thought the price for a new watch was around $100. So, Dubois paid a higher than usual price or else he had bought a better quality watch. I mentioned that the thief might try to hock the watch for $125. Jenkins did say that he was surprised that anyone would steal a new watch with the intention a hocking or selling it."

Richard went on, "I guess watches are fairly plentiful and not too expensive."

"Well, maybe to someone with very little money and unable to hold a job, $125 worth of merchandise is worth stealing," said Alister.

"Ralph Jenkins works at University Computers on Fourth Avenue, downtown," said Richard. "I asked him if anyone was paying much attention to him and Dubois when he was talking to Dubois in the sitting room about his new watch. He said no. Only Dolores Jones and Alfred Johansson were there and Johansson was watching TV."

"OK," said Alister. "Let's start drawing our time line. We can add to it as we go along."

Alister took out two sheets of paper and scotch taped them together. He laid them out on his desk length wise and picked up his pen. He wrote and said, "Monday, September 5, Dubois buys a new wristwatch at Emerald City Diamond for $225."

Alister drew an arrow to the right and wrote and said, "Wednesday, September 7, Dubois shows new watch to David Simmons and Charles Wilson in his room."

Alister drew another arrow to the right and said, "Thursday, September 8, Dubois shows his new watch to Dolores Jones and Ralph Jenkins in the sitting room."

Alister drew another arrow to the right and said, "Saturday, September 10, Dubois goes to Arnold's Broiler and shows his new watch to Janet Smith, Charlene Heath, Jennifer Worthington, and Siegfried Stone."

Alister drew another arrow to the right and said, "Thursday, September 15, Dubois is robbed at 1:00 AM in his room."

Alister stood up, picked up the time chart and went to the cork board on the wall. He pinned the time chart to the cork board. He then took a sheaf of blank pages from his desk, stapled them together, and pinned them to the cork board beneath the time chart. He took his pen and printed on the sheaf of papers "reference material". He then went back to his desk and sat down.

Alister took his notebook out of his pocket, hunted

around in for a bit, and said, "Now it's my turn." He stood up and went to the board. He took out his pen and wrote on the sheaf of papers while saying, "Our arrival at Dubois' apartment revealed a cut on his cheek, probably from being hit by a book end. Also, missing new watch and old emerald ring. The window over the fire escape was forced open."

Alister continued, "Pine Street Clinic. I obtained some bandages from the time of Dubois' visit along with some other bandages. I took the bandages over to Ralph Lee in the blood and fingerprint lab. I also got a sample of Dubois' blood sent to the lab. They identified Dubois' bandages and discovered another blood sample on them. They sent it to the FBI to see if they could identify the DNA of the other person, not Dubois. I haven't got an answer yet."

"Do you think it is Siegfried Stone?" asked Richard.

"It might be him," said Alister. "However, we know that Stone cut his finger in Dubois' room the day before the robbery. So that won't help us."

"It could be somebody else," said Richard. "We're keeping the door open to that."

"Right," said Alister. He paged through his notebook, took up his pen, and wrote on the sheaf of papers while saying, "Interviews. I spoke to Janet Smith, who is Dubois' fiancé, at her apartment. I spoke to Charlene Heath and Jennifer Worthington at Arnold's Broiler. They say Dubois showed them his new watch at Arnold's Broiler. Siegfried Stone showed up at Arnold's Broiler and showed an interest. Nothing special in the interviews with the women."

Alister paged through his notes and continued, "Interview with Siegfried Stone. Stone had a cut on his mouth and a bandage on his hand. Stone says he visited his friend Caspar DuBois a few days before the robbery and cut his finger on a broken cup."

"Did he look like he had been in a fight?" asked Richard.

"A little," answered Alister. "The cut and swollen lip attest to that."

Alister turned back to the cork board. "Now, for our strongest piece of evidence so far. I spoke to James Newton at the forensics lab. He found some black fabric samples lying around the room on the floor."

"That's probably from the scuffle," put in Richard.

"Right," returned Alister. "He took them over to the REI store on Denny and they gave him some samples from their merchandise. Our forensics lab later proved a match between our scraps from Dubois' room and the REI samples."

"That would be a little hard to use in a court room," said Richard.

"Yes, I know," said Alister. "But here is the strongest thing from forensics," said Alister returning to the cork board and writing, "Forensics found a bloody fingerprint on the outside of the metal fire escape. Apparently, the suspect tore his plastic gloves on a rough bracket of the steel fire escape."

"Fantastic!" said Richard. "We have finally got something."

"Yes, indeed," said Alister. "Forensics ran their DNA test on the blood and sent the bloody fingerprints to the FBI in Washington for identification. The result hasn't come back yet."

Alister went back to his desk and sat down. We still have some things we can check while waiting for the FBI."

"We can check the hock shops and secondhand dealers," said Richard. "We are looking for the wrist watch and the emerald ring."

"Did you ask about the supposed California swap meet acquaintance over at Arnold's Broiler?" asked Alister.

"Yes, I did," said Richard. "I went over to Arnold's Broiler this morning while you were over at forensics and asked about him. He does exist and his name is … just a second while I look in my notes." Richard paged through his note book and finally stopped, saying, "Edward Atinsky. The bartender at Arnold's Broiler thinks he lives in the Stuart Building on Denny. I went over there twice. He wasn't home. But the apartment manager said he lives in room 202."

"Well, keep on that. We can check the hock shops on First Avenue and even Highway 99 on the north end. On the south end there's 4th Avenue south."

"I can handle the south end," said Richard.

"All right," said Alister. "I'll start on the north end tomorrow, Wednesday, morning and you can start on the south end."

Alister and Richard sat at their desks and gazed at the timeline.

Alister said, "We know the stolen articles are a wrist watch and an old silver ring with a green emerald inset. The computer difficulty talk between the people involved is just a conversational piece used by Caspar DuBois."

Richard said, "However, as they work together on Dubois' computer and talk amongst themselves, Dubois' new wristwatch is displayed when he reaches for things."

"He even mentions it from time to time," said Alister.

"So, our suspect, Siegfried Stone, sees the ring and even hears that it cost Caspar DuBois $225," put in Richard.

"Now, we have been told that Siegfried Stone has a police record from some other states," Alister mentions. "Therefore, he is cognizant of the manner in which police departments and the FBI work."

"Also, he knows the way courtrooms work and how a jury can be swayed," put in Richard.

"Right," said Alister. "So, suppose he decides to steal the watch and ring, but realizes that a scuffle might ensue and that he might lose some blood or hair in the fight."

Richard interjected, "So, he undertakes to visit his friend and acquaintance, Caspar DuBois, a few days before his planned robbery and manages to cut his finger on something, like a broken coffee cup. This leaves some of his blood in Dubois' apartment. Then, if the police find the blood after the robbery and the FBI identifies it as Stone's blood it will be possible for Stone's lawyer to tell the jury that the blood occurred innocently when Stone cut his finger on a coffee cup."

"Several members of any jury will buy that," said Alister.

"Stone's police record from the past indicates that he had enough experience in trials to think of such a ruse," said Richard.

"However," interjected Alister, "our evidence of the bloody fingerprint on the fire escape can not be explained away in the same manner."

"Exactly," said Richard.

They decided to call it a day and start on the pawn shops the next morning. They put on their coats and left the squad room.

CHAPTER 12

Richard came in early Wednesday morning, September 21. Alister was already at his desk in the cubicle. Richard got on his computer and brought up the usual internet search engine. He typed in "pawn shops Seattle". After surfing around for a while he settled on a group of hock shops and second hand stores on Pacific Highway South, near SeaTac Airport. He wrote down their addresses and shut down his computer.

Richard put on his jacket and got his Glock 9 mm from his desk drawer. He said to Alister, "I've got the addresses of several hock shops on Pacific Highway South near SeaTac. I think I'll check them out."

"OK," said Alister. "I found some here in downtown. I'll check them out this morning."

Richard took the elevator down to the garage and requisitioned an unmarked detective car. He drove out of the station and took the Spring Street entrance onto Highway 5 South. About 45 minutes later he took the SeaTac Airport exit.

After some maneuvering he got onto Pacific Highway South. He drove to his first address, Floyd's Pawn Shop, and parked in front of the building in which the shop was located. Richard walked up to the door of the hock shop and looked at the window display. There were numerous computers and printers and a selection of computer manuals. Over on the far right wall were several musical instruments. Right in front was a tool box containing a lot of hand tools. On the floor around it were various power tools.

Richard went up to the door and walked in. The door had a bell that tinkled when you walked in. The room was dimly lit. Two people were milling about in the far right corner. They were talking to a man in an apron with a badge attached to the front that bore the company logo, Floyd's Pawn Shop.

Richard looked around and started walking up one of the aisles. All of the merchandise was in locked cases with glass tops for viewing. Richard was looking at a case containing electric powered kitchen appliances. Right in front of him was an egg beater.

Richard wondered how the sales process worked. If a customer came in and offered to pay the amount listed on the price tag, could the sales attendant just sell it right then. Or, did the salesperson first have to contact the owner and tell him that he had to repay the hock shop loan amount in 24 hours, or else the hock shop was going to sell the item to the customer who had come in.

The two customers in the corner had apparently finished their business with the salesperson. Richard could see them walking towards the cash register and could hear them having a happy, satisfied conversation.

The customers went out the door and the sales attendant walked towards Richard with a smile and greeting, "Good afternoon, Sir. Can I help you with anything?"

Richard said, "I am a Seattle police detective and I am looking for something." He showed the attendant his police badge, and continued, "We are trying to track down two stolen items."

The attended said, "What are the two items?"

Richard said, "One is a new wrist watch and the other is an old silver ring with a green emerald inset."

The attendant said, "We get lots of rings and wrist watches in here. We never know what property is stolen property when a customer comes in and wants to sell it."

He continued, "Is there some special marking on it?"

Richard answered, "We have the serial number on the watch."

"OK," said the salesperson. "I'll show you the collection of watches and rings that we have."

He led Richard over to a long cabinet with the glass top for viewing the contents. Inside was a large collection of watches.

The sales attendant asked, "What type of watch was it?"

Richard answered, "It is a high quality wrist watch. I don't have any other description of it other than its serial number."

The attended went behind the cabinet, took some keys from his pocket, and opened the cabinet. He reached in and took out two wrist watches and put them on top of the cabinet. He said, "These are the only two high quality wrist watches I have right now."

Richard said, "Would you open the backs of the watches so that I can read the serial numbers, please."

The sales attendant complied.

Richard picked up the first one and turned it over so he

could read the serial number. He got out his notebook and paged through it to the place where he had written Caspar DuBois' watch serial number. After checking the watch in front of him, he said, "This is not the one we're looking for."

He reached for the second watch and made the same check. He said, "This one isn't the one we're looking for either."

"All right," said the store attendant. He returned them to the cabinet.

Richard asked, "Have you sold a wrist watch in the past two weeks?"

The attendant said, "I'll have to check my records."

He headed towards the back of the store and said to Richard, "This way please."

They walked to the back of the shop. The attendant went into a small office and beckoned for Richard to follow. He got out a ledger book and opened it to a place near the back.

"Do you just want to know for the past two weeks?" asked the attendant.

"Yes," answered Richard, "that will be sufficient."

The attendant checked his ledger book and said, "As a matter of fact, we sold one last Saturday."

"Do you have the serial number of that watch?" asked Richard.

"Yes, I do," said the attendant. "We always write down the serial number of things we acquire and keep that serial number in our ledger book after we sell it."

Richard reached for his notebook again and opened it to the page where he had written Caspar DuBois' wristwatch serial number. He said to the attendant, "Would you read the serial number out loud that you have there, please."

The hock shop attendant complied. It was not the same number that Richard had in his notebook.

"Well, that's not the watch we're looking for," said Richard.

Richard paged through his notebook a bit and added, "Have you acquire or sold a silver ring with a green emerald inset recently, Mr. Aldridge? I see you have your name written on the identification plate on your uniform."

Aldridge said, "I'll have to check my computer records again. What time period do you want me to check?"

Richard answered, "The last three weeks."

Presently, Aldridge said, "We bought a silver ring with a green emerald inset eight days ago from Mr. Howard Wellington of 1508 Sunset Drive."

Richard said, "I would like to see it please."

Aldridge led Richard down the aisle on the right almost to the front door. He went behind a cabinet and took some keys out of his pocket to open the cabinet. He reached into the cabinet and moved some rings about and finally came out with a ring that he placed on the counter top. "Here it is," said Aldridge. "We have set a price of $350 on it."

Richard picked up the ring carefully so that he would not smudge any finger prints on it. He turned it so that he could see the inside of the ring band. He had a hard time reading any of the engravings on the ring band. He said, "Do you happen to have a magnifying glass? I'm having a hard time reading these markings."

Aldridge took a magnifying glass from his shirt pocket and handed it to Richard. "Here is the magnifying glass that I use."

Richard took the magnifying glass and said, "Thank

you." Richard took his notebook out of his pocket and turned to the page where he had noted what Dubois had engraved on his ring. Dubois had engraved his initials, CMD, on his ring. When Richard used the magnifying glass to check the ring, he observed the engraving, "With love from Margaret."

Richard returned the ring and said, "This is not the ring we're looking for."

Aldridge put the ring back in the cabinet and locked it.

Richard said, "You don't have either of the items we are looking for. I have another question, not connected with the case."

Aldridge asked, "What is that?"

Richard asked, "Do you have a set of wrenches that are the metric type, calibrated in millimeters not in inches? I have always wanted to buy such a set."

Aldridge responded, "We have one or two sets over here." He led the way to the back of the shop on the right, where most of the tools were located. He stopped at a cabinet and pointed to two sets of wrenches in the cabinet. "Here they are."

Richard looked and noted the price. "I might be in some day to purchase a set," he said, "but not today. They look fine."

Richard said, "Thank you Mr. Aldridge for your time and assistance." He paused a second and then continued, "Just out of curiosity Mr. Aldridge, about how much would a person get in a pawn shop for a new watch that was purchased for $225 a month ago?"

Mr. Aldridge answered, "If it were still in good working order, we would probably give him about a $150 for it."

"When an item is brought in here and the person tries to hock it, do you always check the serial number?" asked Richard.

"Always," answered Aldridge, "but sometimes the serial number is missing or has been partly scraped off. If it is readable, we always compare it against a list of lost merchandise that we can reference on a certain website."

"Some people don't keep the serial numbers of their personal items," said Richard. "They don't always retain the sales slip either."

"So, if the item is lost or stolen, they don't have a serial number to report," Mr. Aldridge said.

"I suppose if someone tries to hock an item that is worth only $50.00 or so, that person must be in pretty dire straits," said Richard.

"Yeah, I suppose that is true," answered Mr. Aldridge. "Either that, or the person just saw something he really wants and it is two weeks to pay day," Aldridge said with a smile.

"Yes, that might be," responded Richard. "Well, thank you for your time, Mr. Aldridge. I'll be on my way. I have another pawn shop to visit this afternoon."

Mr. Aldridge smiled and said, "Good day, detective."

Richard walked out of the shop and over to his car. Just then a navy jet flew over, showing its triangle shaped wings as seen from below. Richard thought that military jets make an enormous amount of noise for their size. He thought that they are not obliged to have mufflers on their engines the way commercial jets are. Mufflers might degrade the performance of the engines, he figured. Or, maybe they just add weight to the airplane he thought.

Richard decided to go to the second hock shop on his list of hockshops to visit. It was still early. He got into his car and got out his notebook. The second hock shop was Jake's Pawn Shop. It was only one mile north of Floyd's Pawn Shop on Pacific Highway South.

When Richard arrived at the address, he turned into the strip mall where the hock shop was located. Richard scanned the shops in the mall and spotted Jake's Pawn Shop without much trouble. He parked in front of the shop.

When Richard entered the establishment he heard the customary bell tinkle over the door. There were two customers in the place. One appeared to be talking with the proprietor behind a glass case.

Richard started walking up one aisle looking at the merchandise in the glass cases. The glass appeared to be shatterproof. Richard could see a wire mesh embedded in the glass. He had noticed when he walked into the shop that a steel bar gate had been rolled back from across the entrance.

The cabinet in front of him contained women's costume jewelry. There were necklaces, bracelets, and watches. The price tag for each item had been turned upside down. You would have to ask the salesperson to show it to you to find out the price.

Richard proceeded to the back of the store, where he saw the selection of tools. When he got there he noticed a selection of garden tools as well as tools for a tool bench. There was a large selection of tools for a tool bench. Richard could imagine a man bringing in a power drill because he needed some money immediately, and then he would have to worry about getting back here after pay day to retrieve his tool before it was sold.

Richard glanced around the entire room. No guns were up for sale. That was good. He knew a gun law had been passed a few years back governing the sale of weapons. Maybe, hock shops were forbidden to sell guns. He heard the doorbell tinkle and noticed that the last customer had just departed. The shop attendant was walking in his direction.

"Good afternoon sir, welcome to Jake's Pawn Shop," the man said.

Richard showed the man his police badge and said, "Good afternoon. I am investigating a robbery that took place on the north end. I am visiting some of the hock shops in town."

The man studied Richard's badge for a moment and asked, "What are you looking for?"

Richard noticed the man had a nameplate on bearing the name Charles. He said, "Charles, I am looking for a wrist watch and a silver ring with a green emerald inset."

Charles answered, "We have quite a few rings and a lot of watches. We have a collection of rings over here," beckoning Richard to follow him.

When they arrived at the cabinet, Richard said, "I am looking for a silver ring with a green emerald inset."

Charles went behind the cabinet. He took a key from his pocket and opened the cabinet. He reached around a bit and came up with two silver rings with green stones. "I have these two," he said.

Richard said, "I would like to examine them carefully. We know there are some initials engraved on the inside of the ring band."

"Certainly," said Charles, as he placed the two rings on the cabinet top.

Richard picked up the first ring and noted that it was indeed a silver ring and had a green emerald inset. He turned the ring over and looked carefully at the inside of the ring band. He could not find Caspar DuBois' initials, CMD.

Richard picked up the second ring. He noted that it was also a silver ring with a green emerald stone embedded in it. He checked the ring band carefully but could not find Dubois' initials on the inside of the ring band.

Richard said, "Neither of these are the ring that I am looking for."

"Sorry," said Charles. He put the two rings back in the cabinet and locked the cabinet door.

"Charles, we are also looking for a high quality wrist watch. Have you purchased one recently?" asked Richard.

Charles answered, "I will have to check my computer." He walked towards his office in the back. "This way please."

When Charles was seated at his desk and ready at his computer, he asked, "What time period are you interested in?"

Richard said, "The last three weeks."

Soon Charles spoke up, "We have several watches and one high quality wrist watch that came in ten days ago. It was brought in by George Custer of 1609 West Union Street.

Richard said, "I would like to see that one."

Charles led the way out of his office and down the aisle to a cabinet on the left. He took out his key from his pocket and opened the back of the cabinet. He reached into the cabinet and pulled out a watch and placed it on the counter.

Richard said, "Could you open the back please so that I

can check the serial number." Charles complied and placed the open watch back on the counter top.

Richard picked it up carefully to avoid smudging any finger prints on it. He had taken out his notebook and turned to the page where he had written Dubois' watch serial number. The serial number on the watch that Charles had handed him and the serial number in his notebook did not match.

"Well, the serial numbers don't match," said Richard. "I guess I will have to search elsewhere." Richard asked, "Do you have many prospective customers come in here on an average day?"

"Oh, quite a few, I would say," answered Charles. "Maybe eight or ten on an average day."

Richard asked him, "How much would a high quality wrist watch or silver ring sell for here?"

Charles answered, "It varies a course, but such a watch would sell for about $150 and a silver ring with emerald inset might sell for $200."

"Not a lot of money," said Richard, "but enough I suppose for a man who finds himself in bad economic straits all of a sudden."

"Yes, that is true," answered Charles.

"Thank you for your time and cooperation, Charles," said Richard. He turned and left the pawn shop.

Richard got back in his car and drove to the entrance to Hwy 5 North. It took him about an hour to drive back downtown to the police station. He left the car in the basement garage and took the elevator up to the squad room.

Alister was not in their cubicle. Richard sat down and stretched a bit. He thought that the trip to the hock shops in the south end was a complete waste. He wondered if Alister had any success in the north end.

Richard turned on his computer and proceeded to update his records of the case. He wondered how long it would be before the lieutenant told them to set aside the DuBois case because he had a more serious case for them to work on.

Chapter 13

Alister started his visit of the hock shops at 10:30 AM on Wednesday, September 21. Before leaving the police station he checked the list of addresses of hock shops that the police department kept. He also checked the telephone Yellow Pages. After compiling a list, he decided to start his investigation on First Avenue in Pioneer Square and move north.

There wasn't any advantaged in having a vehicle along. The entire trek only covered about one mile on First and Second avenues. Besides, the weather was nice. So, he decided to walk. Alister put on his jacket. He took his Glock 9 mm out of his desk drawer and put it in his shoulder holster. He took the elevator down and emerged on Fourth Avenue.

He walked over to First Avenue and headed for his first hock shop. Pioneer Square was fairly busy. A lot of people were patronizing the shops in the area. Another huge group were sitting on benches in the park. Alister's first hock shop had Pioneer Square Pawn Shop written in gold letters on the window. The steel bar gate had been drawn back from the entrance. Alister stopped for a minute to gaze at the merchandise on display in the window. There were some computers and sound systems on display. There were a few music instruments there. A nicely bound collection of books was in a box. A few electric kitchen appliances were on display.

Alister went to the door and entered. Four or five groups of people were milling about. Presumably, a sales attendant was in some of the groups. The single room was of medium size. There were pictures on the walls; some had fancy frames. Alister wondered if they had been pawned by someone or were they just decorations that the shop owner had purchased.

After about half an hour, only two groups remained in the room. Alister guessed that they were discussing prices. The others had departed.

Alister stepped over to a glass cabinet containing power tools. There were a couple of electric drills and a jig saw. A socket wrench set was there.

Alister heard the door chimes sound and turned to see one customer exit. The shop attendant who had been speaking to the customer was now walking in Alister's direction.

"Hello," said the man with a smile on his face. His name badge displayed the name Eric. Eric wore prominent dark red colored suspenders holding up his dark trousers. He wore a white shirt with a bow-tie. Alister hadn't seen a bow-tie in ages. He wondered if Eric had to tie it every morning or was it a snap on tie. Eric wore dark horn rim glasses. Altogether, he stood out in public.

"Hello, Eric," said Alister. Alister showed the man his police badge and continued, "We are investigating a robbery, and I am looking for a few items that somebody might have hocked."

Eric checked Alister's badge and asked, "What items?"

Alister answered, "I am looking for a high quality wrist watch and a silver ring with a green emerald inset."

Eric said, "Our watches are this way," gesturing towards the left side of the shop. "If you will come this way, please."

They stopped at a cabinet that contained many watches. Eric went behind the cabinet and unlocked the cabinet door. He reached in and took out a watch. He said, "This is the only high quality wrist watch we have. I will have to go to the office to check the records to find out when it came in. Will you follow me please?"

Eric led the way to the back of the shop and Alister followed. They entered a small room containing a desk and a chair. There was a steel book case holding several record books or ledgers. Eric took down a ledger and opened it on the desk. He checked the watch he held in his hand for the hock shop's item number that had been printed on it and then consulted the ledger. He found it in a printout and said, "We acquired his watch eight days ago."

Alister said, "Could you open the back of the watch and read out the serial number?"

Eric looked for the serial number while Alister paged through his notebook to find the serial number of Dubois' wristwatch.

Eric said, "Here it is. Are you ready?"

Alister said, "Go ahead."

Eric read the number out loud and Alister compared it against the number in his notebook.

Alister said, "Wrong number."

Eric responded, "That's the only high quality wrist watch we have. Sorry."

Alister responded, "We are also looking for a silver ring with a green emerald inset. We have the inscription that is engraved on the ring band."

Eric put away the ledger and said, "Let's go look at our ring collection."

They both left the office and Eric led Alister to the cabinet where they had their rings on display. Along the way to it, Eric put the watch back in its cabinet. Eric went behind the ring cabinet and used his key to open it. He examined his collection and drew out one ring.

Eric said, "This is the only silver ring with green emerald inset that I have," holding the ring up for to Alister to see.

Alister said, "I guess we will have to go back to your office and check your records to find out when the ring came in."

"Certainly," said Eric closing and locking the cabinet.

They went back to the office. Eric took a ledger book off the shelf on the wall and sat down at his desk. After a moment he found what he was looking for. Eric said, "We acquired the ring six days ago."

Alister said, "May I inspect the ring closely. We know there's a certain inscription on the inside of the ring band." Alister checked the ring band carefully but could not find Caspar DuBois' initials, CMD, on the ring. He said, "I cannot find the inscription that I am looking for." Alister said, "Thanks for your time, but I will have to look elsewhere."

They left the office and proceeded towards the front door.

Alister asked, "Are the pictures on the walls pawned items. Are they for sale? I noticed them before when I was standing here waiting for you."

Eric answered, "Yes, they are pictures that people brought in here to put in hock. And, yes, they are for sale."

Alister asked, "If a customer wanted to buy one could you just sell it, or do you have to telephone the owner and give him a certain number of days to buy it back first?"

"We have to call the owner first," answered Eric.

Alister said, "I guess some people can get into financial straits and have to pawn something until pay day."

Eric answered, "Yes, quite a few people find themselves in that position occasionally."

Alister responded, "I've never had a friend or relative who pawned anything."

Eric laughed a bit. "Well, count yourself fortunate," he said.

Alister thanked Eric again for his time and left. He checked his watch and saw that it was 11:45 AM. He decided that he had time to visit another pawnshop. He got out his list of pawn shops and ran down the list. He decided that he would try "Elmer's Pawnshop" next. It wasn't far away. He looked around a bit to get his bearings and set out.

It was a pleasant day and a lot of people were sitting in the park that the city had constructed there, and maintains.

Alister noticed a lot of young people apparently in their twenties and thirties. He always thought that there was something wrong with this situation. When he went into the grocery store that he typically used, he heard the store staff mention over the loudspeaker system that there were jobs available. There was a sign in the aisle that advertised jobs.

Alister thought surely it is preferable to work in a grocery store than to just sit around and wait for a handout. He, of course, thought some of these people had worked in that environment and had got laid off several times. Maybe their employment record causes an employment manager to be disinclined to hire them again.

Alister proceeded up the street. The city keeps Pioneer Square looking pretty clean and attractive. Of course, it is a tourist attraction and the city wants to accommodate the tourist industry.

According to the address Alister had of Elmer's Pawnshop, it ought to be on First Avenue near Columbia Street. He was approaching Columbia now, and started looking for Elmer's Pawnshop. At 12:05 PM, Alister found the shop; it was the third shop on First Avenue north of Columbia Street. It displayed its name, Elmer's Pawn Shop, in gold letters on its window behind sturdy looking steel bars covering the entire window expanse. Alister entered and set off the entry bell. He proceeded to the back of the store down a fairly narrow aisle between several display cases holding watches, bracelets, music instruments, several laptop computers, and assorted other things. He expected to see a lot of hand guns for sale. But the new laws required that the proprietor of a shop must take the finger prints of a person trying to buy a gun and send them to the FBI. If the FBI sends a report back the next day saying the prospective buyer is not a criminal, then the person can buy the gun the following day.

A man, who had been sitting in a cage made of steel bars at the back of the store, heard the door chime that Alister had set off. He came forward and said, "Good afternoon, sir, may I help you?"

Alister took out his badge and showed it to him. "I am detective Alister Jensen of the Seattle police department," he said.

The man looked at Alister's badge and said, "What can I do for you, detective?"

"I am investigating a robbery that occurred on Thursday, September 15," said Alister.

May I have your name, sir?"

"My name is Patrick Weiman," said the man. "My father's name was Elmer."

"I am glad to meet you, Patrick," said Alister.

"OK," answered Patrick. "The robbery you mentioned occurred a little over a week ago."

"Yes," returned Alister. "I am looking for a high quality wrist watch and a silver ring with a green emerald inset."

Patrick answered, "Let's go back to my office and check if any rings came in during the past three weeks."

They proceeded to Patrick Weiman's office in the rear of the store. Patrick sat down at his desk and busied himself with his computer. After a few minutes he asked, "Do you have a description of the ring?"

Alister answered, "It is a silver ring with a green emerald inset."

Patrick checked his computer again and announced, "We acquired a ring with a jewel inset one week ago. It was brought in by a Mr. Dale Ferguson of 1507 Madison Street."

Alister responded, "I would like to see it."

They left the office and proceeded down the second aisle to a glass case containing a great many rings. Patrick went behind the case and took out his key from his pocket and opened the case. He reached into the case and after moving some rings around for a minute, he took out one and placed it on top of the counter. "Here it is," Patrick said. "The price on it is $150."

Alister picked up the ring and examined it carefully. He noticed some marks on the inside of the ring band. He asked, "Do you have a magnifying glass? I am looking for a certain inscription."

Patrick took a small magnifying glass from his vest pocket and handed it to Alister.

Alister accepted the magnifying glass and said, "Thank you." He took his notebook from his coat pocket and turned to his note on the Dubois' ring. Dubois had said that his initials, CMD, are on the inside of the ring band. Alister examine the inscription on the ring band and decided it was not the initials, CMD.

Alister said, "This is not the ring we're looking for."

He returned the ring to Patrick Weiman.

"I haven't seen many silver rings with green emerald insets," said Patrick, "but watches come and go almost every day."

"All right," said Alister. "I would like to look at your supply of recently acquired watches.

"I'll checked my inventory," said Patrick.

He went back into his cage and started paging through a book or ledger. Presently, Patrick announced, "We bought a high quality wrist watch on September 16 for $150."

"I would like to see it please," said Alister.

Patrick came out of his cage and proceeded down the aisle to a display counter. He went behind the counter and opened it with a key he had taken from his pocket. He reached in and took out a watch and placed it on the counter. "Here it is," said Patrick. "We bought it from a Mr. Orville Reinhardt on September 16 for $100. He gave his address as 1605 First Avenue, apartment 208."

"How often do people come back to retrieve the item they pawned by buying it back?" asked Alister.

"Oh, about one third of the time I would say," answered Patrick. "Usually, they have a hard time acquiring the money to buy it back. That's why they pawned it in the first place."

Alister very carefully handled the watch. He didn't want to put any more finger prints than necessary on it. He asked, "Is there a serial number on this?"

"I have to pry open the lid on the back to see the serial number," answered Patrick.

Alister gave him the watch and Patrick opened the back of it.

Alister took out his notebook and turned to the page where he had written down the serial number of DuBois' watch.

Before leaving the police station on his trip to the pawn shops, Alister had called forensics and asked Newton if police headquarters had the sales slip that Caspar DuBois had used to buy his watch. Newton had checked his records and said that they did have the sales slip. Alister had then asked Newton to read the serial number off the sales slip while he wrote it down in his note book.

Now while standing in Elmer's Pawn Shop, Alister compared the serial number on the back of the watch that Patrick was holding with the serial number he had written in his notebook. They did not match.

Alister said, "Patrick, the numbers don't match. Thank you, Patrick, for your cooperation."

Alister thanked Patrick for his time and assistance and left the shop.

CHAPTER 14

Alister stepped out of Elmer's Pawnshop and looked at his watch. It was 12:15 PM. He decided that he had time for one more pawnshop. He took out the list of pawn shops he had made before leaving the police station. He decided he would try First Avenue Pawnshop. Its address was on First Avenue near Union Street.

When he got there, he noticed it was quite small. It had a small window display behind steel bars. There were some wristwatches, a few bracelets, and several power tools on display.

Alister entered the store and proceeded down the single central aisle. The proprietor was conferring with a customer on the left, towards the rear.

Alister stopped at the counter on the right and gazed at the assortment of the electric tools in the case. Several electric drills and wrench sets were on display.

Presently the customer completed his businesses and left the store. The proprietor came up to Alister and said, "Good afternoon, sir. Welcome to First Avenue Pawnshop."

Alister said, "Good afternoon. I am a Seattle police detective looking for a couple of stolen items." He showed his badge to the proprietor and asked, "Could I have your name?"

The proprietor looked at Alister's badge and said, "My name is Edward Norton. What items are you looking for?"

Alister answered, "I am looking for a high quality wrist watch and a silver ring with a green emerald inset."

Edward said, "Please come back to my office where I keep my records." He led the way to the back of the store where there was a small office containing a desk and chair with a computer on the desk. After Edward sat down and started up his computer, he asked, "At what date do you want me to start looking?"

Alister answered, "Just check your records for the past three weeks."

Edward consulted his computer again and said, "A high quality wrist watch came in last week but no rings have come in for over a month."

Alister said, "I would like to see the watch, please."

Edward rose and led Alister down the aisle to a display case near the door. He went behind the case and took a key from his pocket to unlock the case. He reached in the case and after moving some watches around, selected one and brought it out of the case and put it on the counter.

"This watch was brought in last Monday by a Mr. Ralph Sommers," Edward said.

Alister said, "Would you opened the back please so that I can see the serial number."

Edward picked up the watch and using a pen knife that he took from his pocket, he opened the back of the watch. He handed the watch to Alister.

Alister took his notebook from his jacket and opened it

to the record of the watch serial number. The serial number on the watch handed to him by Edward Norton did not match the serial number in his notebook.

Alister said, "This is not the watch we are looking for." He handed the watch back to Edward. "Thank you very much for your time and assistance, Mr. Edward Norton. We will have to look elsewhere."

Alister left the pawn shop and decided it was time to return to the police station.

Alister had come on foot since he knew he would be going to a lot of hock shops and did not want the nuisance of constantly parking and moving the squad car.

He walked up Seneca from First to Fifth Avenue. Seneca was a very steeply inclined street. Alister always figured that if you worked downtown and had to use Seneca or Union much, you would eventually develop some very strong and healthy lungs.

When Alister got back to the police station, he took the elevator up to the squad room. Alister went back to his cubicle and spent an hour updating his computer record of the case. He described his visits to the pawn shops and lack of success in that venture. Richard came in to the cubicle while Alister was working on his computer.

"Hi," said Richard. "I see you're back from checking your hock shops. I just finished mine, also."

"Hi, Richard," said Alister. "Why don't you update your computer records while I go downstairs to Randolphs and get a coffee. Do you want one? I can bring one up for you."

"Sure," said Richard. "I'll take an Espresso. Thanks."

Alister took the elevator down to the lobby. Margaret was working at the Randolphs stand. "Hello, Margaret,

I would like an Espresso and an Americano, please," said Alister.

"Hi, Alister," said Margaret. She set about making his two coffees.

When Alister got back upstairs to the cubicle with the two coffees, Richard was just completing the update of his computer records. Alister set Richard's Espresso on his desk and then sat down at his own desk.

Alister said, "Let us discuss our visits to the hock shops before going home. Why don't you start?"

Richard began, "OK. I visited two hock shops down near SeaTac airport. The first one was 'Floyd's Pawn Shop' on Pacific Highway South. They had a wrist watch but it had the wrong serial number. They also had a silver ring with green emerald inset, but it had the wrong inscription."

Alister interjected, "I had similar results."

Richard continued, "The next hock shop I visited was 'Jakes Pawn Shop' on Pacific Highway South. They had a wrist watch with a serial number different from the one we are looking for. Also, they had a silver ring with emerald inset. But, it had an inscription different from the one we are looking for."

"Discouraging, isn't it?" said Alister.

Richard responded, "There must be at least fifty pawn shops in Seattle. We can't visit them all."

"No, of course not," responded Alister. "It is hard to guess the right ones to visit."

"I regarded my investigation of pawn shops as a total loss," said Richard.

Alister began his account. "I visited three hock shops downtown. I went first to 'Pioneer Square Pawn Shop' on

First Avenue. They had a wrist watch but it didn't have the serial number we are looking for. They also had a silver ring with green emerald inset, but it didn't have the inscription we are looking for. I visited next 'Elmer's Pawn Shop' on First Avenue. Same thing there. They had a wrist watch with the wrong serial number and a silver ring with emerald inset. But, the ring had an inscription different from the one we are looking for. The third pawn shop I went to was 'First Avenue Pawn Shop' on First Avenue. They didn't have a silver ring with emerald inset but they did have a wrist watch. However, it had a different serial number than we are looking for."

"It looks like a total loss for both of us," said Richard.

"Yeah, there are just too many hock shops in town to check out," said Alister.

"Well. I guess we had to try it," said Richard.

"Maybe, we will do better with the DNA tests on the blood samples we found," said Alister.

"The personal interviews with people Caspar DuBois knew yield some clues also," remarked Richard.

They decided to quit for the day.

Alister stopped at the grocery store on his way home that night. Alister wasn't much of a cook. For him, cooking with just the chore you have to go through if you want to eat properly. If you ate at restaurants too often, you would probably get too much salt and fat. Salt and fat are what give flavor to a dish and restaurants want to sell their cuisine. So, Alister had bought a cookbook and was going through it, trying things. He had had quite a problem at the bookstore deciding on which cook book to buy.

He didn't want a cookbook that described recipes for

fancy haute cuisine dishes with lots of different spices. He just wanted a cookbook that described common or ordinary dishes with limited seasonings and spices. Alister just needed a cookbook that gave you simple recipes and told you how many minutes to leave a dish in the oven and what temperature to use. Or, how long to simmer it on the stove. He didn't want to get sick from inadequately cooked meat dishes.

Today, he had planned just an ordinary baked pot roast. Last night, Alister had found a recipe in his cook book for a five pound pot roast. He had written down on a grocery list any spices that he didn't have.

When Alister got to the meat department he didn't have much trouble finding a nice looking five pound piece of beef. He went to the produce department and found a yellow onion, a clove of garlic, two potatoes for baking, a package of carrots, and a bunch of celery. Over in the spice department he found some extra virgin olive oil. The rest of the spices he already had at home. He just picked up the remaining things on his grocery list and was ready to leave.

It was a pleasant drive home. The sky was blue for a change and the mountains were out. The weather had been clear for several days now.

When he got home, he put the groceries on the kitchen sink, put on some music, and opened the door to the patio to let some fresh air in.

He then returned to the kitchen for what he figured would be a two hour cooking project. He got out his cook book, turned to the recipe for roast beef, and launched into the project.

After dinner, he watched the 11 PM news report on TV.

Alister always thought that the 11:00 PM news report was to a considerable extent the daily police report.

Alister arrived at work early the next morning. He stopped at the Randolphs in the lobby for a coffee to get pumped up for the day. When he got off the elevator, he noticed that Richard was already in the cubicle working on his computer.

"Good morning, Richard," Alister said.

Richard looked up from his computer and said, "Hi, Alister."

Alister said, "Well our investigation of the pawn shops in the north end and south end yielded nothing yesterday."

"I think I'll head over to Atinsky's apartment before he leaves for the day," said Richard.

Alister said, "I think I will have a talk with Ralph Lee and James Newton in forensics. I want to go over all our evidence and make sure we didn't miss something and jump too soon to the conclusion that Siegfried Stone is our suspect. I'll also re-read my notes from interviewing the people at Arnold's Broiler."

"Yeah," it's always a possibility that we chose a suspect too soon. We can't do much until the fingerprint analysis on the fire escape comes back from the FBI," said Richard.

"I keep wondering about DuBois' comment about his assailant carrying a bag," said Alister.

"Maybe he brought the bag in with him," said Richard.

Alister said, "When you get back from seeing Atinsky, or back from California to pick up the watch and ring if Atinsky's interview leads you there, we can both go over to the REI camping store with Stone's photograph. Maybe we can find the salesperson who sold the ski outfit to Stone.

Alister realized that even if Richard does locate the watch and silver ring through the California swap meet person, it might not help. Just fingerprints on the watch or ring won't do much. Stone and Dubois were acquaintances and Stone visited Dubois in his apartment from time to time. A pawnshop proprietor's or a swap meet buyer's witness testimony in court might not carry much weight, if the witness is not certain or sure of his identification.

Richard set out from the office at 1:00 PM to interview Edward Atinsky, the man who frequents swap meets in California. Richard had been to his apartment twice, but he wasn't home. The manager of his apartment building on Denny said that Atinsky definitely lived there.

Richard checked out an unmarked police car in the basement garage of the police station. He headed up Sixth Avenue towards Denny Street. The Stuart building was a three story brick building. The entranceway might have been fairly elegant sixty years ago, but the bushes were untrimmed now and the windows hadn't been washed in months.

The Stuart building, where Atinsky lived, was originally an elegant structure. It was a three story brick building with white marble facing. The windows had leaded glass panes that were very handsome. The view was of the Sound, with the Seattle Center in sight.

In the ensuing years, many commercial buildings and warehouses had been built in the area. The Stuart building was still stately and handsome but the landscaping and the cleanliness had been allowed to decline.

Richard went up to the front door and entered the vestibule of the building. He found the manager's apartment in the list of tenants on the wall to the left. He pressed the manager's apartment button and waited. After a minute someone said, "Manager speaking."

Richard spoke into the mike, "This is Richard Hopkins with the Seattle police. I spoke to you last week."

After a moment, the bell sounded and the door latch was released. Richard entered and proceeded to the manager's apartment, apartment 101. Richard knocked on the door and waited. Soon the door opened and the manager looked out. He said, "Good afternoon, detective Hopkins. Back again?"

"Yes," said Richard. "Edward Atinsky wasn't home the last time I was here. I'll just try his door again." He smiled and walked down the hall.

Richard knocked on the door of apartment 202. He could hear a radio or TV on inside. After a minute the door opened and an unshaven man, about 45 years old, looked out. "Yes?" he said.

Richard held up his badge and said, "Richard Hopkins, Seattle police department. I am looking for Edward Atinsky."

The man answered, "I am Edward Atinsky. What do you want?"

Edward Atinsky was a stooped, thin man. He had on a bathrobe and slippers. He had evidently been in the bathroom about to take a shower when Richard had knocked on the door.

Richard said, "I am investigating the robbery of Caspar DuBois. This is just a routine visit with the people who Caspar DuBois knew. I think you were acquainted with Siegfried Stone who was a friend of Dubois. May I come in and speak with you?"

Atinsky stood aside and waved Richard in. "All right," he said, "I know Stone; we have business dealings occasionally." He closed the door behind him and continued, "I never spoke to Dubois. I might have seen him at Arnold's Broiler once or twice."

His apartment was dimly lit due to the fact that the blinds at the windows were nearly drawn shut. There were magazines strewn about on chairs. A newspaper lay open on the table in front of the couch. A couple of beer cans or pop cans were sitting next to the newspaper.

There was a couch and two chairs in the living room and a table and chairs in the kitchen, which Richard could see through an alcove.

"Would you like to sit down, detective Hopkins?" asked Atinsky.

"Thank you," said Richard. He sat in the chair that matched the couch.

Atinsky sat on the couch.

"Mr. Atinsky, may I ask what your business relations with Mr. Stone are?" asked Richard.

"Stone buys things at pawn shops, garage sales, and secondhand shops. He sells some of these things to me and I take them down to California and try to sell them at swap meets at a marked up price," answered Atinsky.

"Have you been to California, recently?" asked Richard.

"Yes, as a matter of fact," answered Atinsky. "I just returned last night."

"I am interested in a certain wrist watch and a silver ring with a green emerald inset," said Richard. "Did you take a wrist watch or an emerald ring down there recently?"

After a moment Atinsky answered, "Yes, I did."

"Did you manage to sell either one?" asked Richard.

Atinsky answered, "Yes, I did. As a matter of fact I sold both of them."

Atinsky was obviously agitated and worried. If a police officer goes to his home and asks questions about merchandise he handled, there was the possibility that the merchandise was stolen property.

"Do you have a record of who bought those things?" asked Richard.

"Just a minute," said Atinsky. "I'll have to check my records."

He went to a desk and took a ledger from the desk drawer. He paged through it and presently said, "I sold the watch to Clarence Bourdeau. He runs an automobile repair shop in Fresno."

Atinsky paged through his ledger again, running his finger down a column. After a minute he said, "I sold the ring to Orville Svensen. He also lives in Fresno, California and works at Golden State Real Estate."

"Do you have the sales price recorded there? Of course, you don't have to answer that," said Richard.

Atinsky consulted the ledger and said, "I sold the ring for $325." He paged back in the ledger to the watch entry, and said, "I sold the watch for $150."

"A California swap meet frequently occurs on a large tract of land. It can be an outdoor bazaar. Booths are set up and are rented to the people selling goods. A seller can also just display his goods on a portable rack or in a tent," said Atinsky.

Atinsky continued, "I sold the watch on the second day to Clarence Bourdeau."

Richard asked, "Did many people look at the watch the first day you where there?"

"Oh, yes," answered Atinsky, "a great many people looked at it. But I listed it at a fairly high price."

"I sold the silver ring with green emerald inset to Orville Svensen the fourth day I was there," continued Atinsky.

"Did you ask a high price for that also?" asked Richard.

"Certainly," answered Atinsky. "It is a very handsome ring."

"I figured I could get a good price. A great many people go to the fairs. The weather is fine, and the people flock to the swap meets like they are outdoor fairs."

"I suppose some people go to these swap meets on a regular basis," said Richard.

"They do," returned Atinsky.

Richard said, "If Clarence Bourdeau runs an automobile repair company, I suppose he would be at his repair shop almost every day."

Atinsky agreed, "I suppose so."

Richard continued, "It might be more difficult to reach Orville Svensen if he works in a real estate company."

"Possibly," said Atinsky.

"Does your ledger book, there, tell you who sold you the wrist watch and emerald ring?" asked Richard.

Atinsky was quite ill at ease and worried at this point. He evidently felt that it was better for him to tell the truth and not withhold evidence.

Atinsky looked at the ledger book again and said, "I bought the watch from Siegfried Stone for $80.00."

He then paged back to the emerald ring entry and said,

"I bought the emerald ring from Siegfried Stone, also, for $275.00"

Richard said, "Thank you Mr. Atinsky. You have been helpful." Richard rose and moved toward the door. He turned and asked, "Mr. Atinsky, do you know the name of Mr. Bourdeau's automobile repair shop?"

Atinsky closed his ledger book and reached into his desk drawer. He pulled out a small box of business cards and started leaving through them. After a couple of minutes he said, "Here it is, Fresno Motors. At 1502 Sunrise Road." Atinsky continued looking through his box of business cards. Presently, he said, "I've got the second one. Golden State Real Estate. It has Orville Svensen's name on. The address is 902 Hillside Avenue, Fresno, California."

Richard wrote the information in his notebook and said, "Thank you Mr. Atinsky. I'll be leaving now."

CHAPTER 15

When Richard got to his unmarked police car, he decided it was early enough in the day for him to return to the office and request travel authorization to Fresno, California. As he drove toward the police station, he composed the argument he would use for requesting travel authorization.

Richard checked in his car at the car keys station in the basement of the police station and took the elevator to the squad room on the third floor. Alister was not in the cubicle.

Richard proceeded to the lieutenant's office. The door was open and the lieutenant was at his desk. Richard knocked once on the door and stepped in.

Lieutenant Adams said, "Detective Hopkins. Come on in."

"Good afternoon, lieutenant," said Richard. "I think I have located the wrist watch and silver ring with emerald inset that was stolen from Caspar DuBois. I just need to go down to California and expropriate it. I have interviewed a man here in town who we think sold the watch to the owner of an automobile repair shop in Fresno and the ring to a man who works in a real estate office in Fresno."

Lieutenant Adams took out the budget book from his

desk and consulted it. After a few moments, he said, "All right. It appears we have funds for a travel voucher."

Richard said, "Thank you, lieutenant," and went back to his desk. Richard picked up the telephone and dialed their secretary, Stephanie's, number.

When she answered, Richard said, "Hi Stephanie. This is Richard Hopkins. Could you book me on a morning flight tomorrow to Fresno, California? I'll probably be coming back a couple days later."

Richard then took out a travel voucher form and set to filling it out. About 20 minutes later, Stephanie telephoned to say that she had booked the 9:30 AM flight from SeaTac. He would be staying at the Holiday Inn at the Airport and there was also a Hertz rental car awaiting him.

Richard was just about done filling out the travel voucher when Alister walked into the cubicle. "How are things going?" asked Alister when he sat down.

"I think I have located the wrist watch and the ring down in Fresno, California," said Richard. "I got to talk to Edward Atinsky today, and he is cooperating."

"Good," said Alister.

"I just filled out the travel voucher to Fresno," said Richard. When I get back we can check the serial number on the watch and the initials that DuBois scratched on the inside of the ring band to identify them."

"That ought to work," said Alister.

When Richard got home that night his wife, Melanie, was in the kitchen preparing supper.

"Hi Richard," she said when he walked into the kitchen. "You are home a little earlier than usual tonight, aren't you?" she said looking at the clock on the wall.

"Yes," answered Richard. "I will be going down to Fresno, California on a one or two day assignment tomorrow. So, I'll need to pack a little."

Melanie was used to these sudden trips to other cities, but she didn't like it. First of all, she thought police work was way too dangerous. Why couldn't men just accept ordinary jobs.

"Is your partner, Alister, going with you?" she asked.

"No," answered Richard. "I am just going down to Fresno to pick up a watch and a ring. I already know where they are. The owner of an automobile repair shop in Fresno just bought the watch and a real estate agent in Fresno just bought the ring.

Richard knew that Melanie was always worried about his safety. Melanie was a college school teacher. She taught chemistry.

"How did things go today at school?" he asked, to change the subject.

"Oh, all right. Our class took a trip to Allied Chemical today to view their labs and working conditions." she said.

"What do they make at Allied Chemical?" asked Richard.

"Lots of things. One of their products is a fertilizer that puts potassium back in the soil after years of farming," Melanie said. "We are studying fertilizers right now."

"Did they give you a tour of the plant to show you the process?" asked Richard.

"Yes, they provided a very nice and complete tour of one of their fertilizer production lines," said Melanie. "They have some very expensive and up to date machines there."

"Fine," said Richard. "So, what's for dinner tonight?"

"I made chili," said Melanie. "I used some of the chili powder that I bought in bulk at the grocery store. I've got two cups of kidney beans; I soaked them overnight. Also, I've got one cup of pinto beans. I also tossed in some chopped up garlic cloves and a chopped up jalapeno pepper."

"Sounds great," said Richard.

Just then Rachel came into the kitchen. "Hi, daddy!" she said.

"Hi, Rachel," returned Richard. "Have you been using your new scooter much?"

"Yes," answered Rachel. "Marguerite and I rode our scooters down to the park today."

"You watch out carefully when you cross 83rd Street, Rachel," said Richard. "You have to look both directions and pay close attention to the cars when you cross. Remember, you should get off your scooter and carry it in your hand when you cross the street."

"We do," said Rachel.

"Wash your hands, now, Rachel," said Melanie. "Supper will be ready in just a couple of minutes."

After a few moments, Melanie asked Richard, "What time do you have to leave tomorrow?"

"My plane leaves SeaTac at 9:30 AM," answered Richard. "So, I guess I have to get there at 8:00 AM." He paused a minute and continued, "I'll set the alarm for 6:00 AM."

Rachel came back into the kitchen and sat in her chair at the table and they started supper.

The check in line at the Airport the next morning had an aisle leading off to the right with the sign 'Foreign and Domestic Government Officials' above it. Richard went down that aisle and walked up to the counter that was straight ahead. The one person at the counter was just completing his business, speaking in French. When he left, Richard stepped forward and presented his police badge. He said, "I have a 9 mm Glock to declare. I am carrying it in a holster under my left arm."

The attendant checked Richard's badge number, typed something into his computer, and said, "Please open your jacket so that I can see the gun."

Richard did as he was instructed.

After a few moments the attendant looked at his computer again and said, "All right detective Hopkins. I'll print out a card for you to show the flight attendant when you board the airplane."

A second later, the attendant reached over to his printer to retrieve Richard's pass and handed it to him.

"You can proceed through that door, indicating a door in the room, to the loading area," said the attendant.

Richard proceeded to the airplane loading area through the door. He did not have to take the usual passenger loading route with its x-ray detectors and attendants who search your clothing.

Richard's plane landed at Fresno Airport at 11:00 AM. Richard made his way to the baggage room and picked up his bag off the carousel. He appreciated the pleasant weather as he walked over to the car rental office. It was in a small building adjacent to the airport. He took out his car rental receipt that Stephanie had given him at the office along with his airline ticket.

The automobile attendant looked at his ticket and then checked his computer. "We've got a Ford or a Honda," he said. "Which do you prefer?"

Richard said, "I'll take the Ford."

After signing the papers, Richard asked for a map of the town so he could find his way about. Ten minutes later, Richard drove into the Holiday Inn at the Airport where Stephanie had booked a room for him. After Richard was settled in his single room he took the elevator to the top floor where there were a restaurant and cafeteria that overlooked the entire area.

Richard chose chicken salad and coffee for lunch. He looked out the windows while waiting for his lunch. He presumed he was looking east because there was a huge mountain range before him. He figured if he were looking west he would see smaller mountains or hills along the coastline. The Pacific Ocean was about 110 miles to the west.

The waitress arrived with his lunch. The chicken salad was delicious. He decided to drink at least one cup of coffee because he had a big day ahead of him and he wanted to stay alert.

He got out his map while still sitting at the table. He folded it carefully so that he didn't make a spectacle of himself sitting at his table reading a map. The Airport was several miles from Fresno. Fresno was a city of over 500,000 people and he had to study the map carefully to find Sunrise Road. He finally found it and figured out which road or highway to use to get there. He paid his restaurant bill, left a tip for the waitress, and set out for 1502 Sunrise Road.

He found the automobile repair shop quite easily. It was painted red with green trim. It bore the sign 'Fresno Motors' with an automatic rotating light advertising display indicating that brake repairs were currently on special sale at $89.00 plus parts. Richard drove around the block and then drove into the lot. He parked in a vacant parking place on the left.

The large garage door had been rolled up, so Richard just entered and looked around. There was a car up on a hoist to the left. A mechanic was standing in a pit under the car working on something. The car looked like it was a fairly new green Porche. Straight ahead of him was a white car with its hood up and a mechanic leaning into it, working on the motor. To the right was a doorway. Richard could see a desk in the room and a man sitting at the desk. He decided it was the office and walked towards it.

"Good afternoon," said Richard. "I am looking for a Mr. Clarence Bourdeau."

The man at the desk said, "I'm Clarence Bourdeau. What can I do for you?"

The man had on the usual grey coveralls worn in machine shops and automobile repair garages. It had the company logo, Fresno Motors, in a bold red emblem at the top, on the left. He was probably about 40 years old. He was a little over 6 feet tall and of a stocky, sturdy build. He had light brown hair which he kept in a brush haircut, or athlete's hair cut. He had a trim mustache and a short trim beard. He wore eyeglasses. He had an abrupt, gruff manner. He gave the impression of a person who felt he was engaged in hard, important work and was annoyed by people who interrupted him.

"My name is Richard Hopkins. I am not here to have my car fixed. I just came down from Seattle. I am a detective from the Seattle police department," said Richard. Richard showed his badge to Clarence Bourdeau.

Bourdeau looked carefully at his badge and said, "What do you want?"

Richard said, "I am working on a robbery case and have to interview anyone who was acquainted with the victim. While conducting a routine interview with Mr. Edward Atinsky in Seattle, we found out that he was down here in California at a swap meet recently and sold a wrist watch to you."

"Yeah, I bought a wrist watch here a week ago at a swap meet," said Bourdeau. "I don't know if the watch was connected with some robbery in Seattle," said Bourdeau. "There is a ton of stuff sold at those swap meets. Some of it is acquired at garage sales or secondhand stores in some town and sold at a swap meet at a mark-up."

"Yes, I understand that," said Richard. "There is no way for a prospective buyer at a swap meet to know whether the item was stolen two months before or not. But the police have to investigate robberies."

"We have been tracking a stolen wrist watch for about a week," continued Richard. "A man who is a resident of Seattle was attacked in his home in Seattle about a week ago. The attack occurred at night. The victim got in a fight with his assailant. Fingerprints were deposited around the site where the fight developed. Also, some drops of blood were shed. The police sent the blood drops to the FBI to see if they could identify the intruder from his DNA. So, the police have fingerprints and DNA. During their investigation, the police came across a man who lives in Seattle and travels to California swap meets to sell goods he purchases at garage sales and secondhand stores in Seattle. This man, who travels to California swap meets, purchased a watch from an acquaintance in Seattle and brought it down here to sell. He keeps accurate records of these transactions and claims he sold a wrist watch to you several days ago."

"Wrist watches have serial numbers if they haven't been filed off," continued Richard.

"So, I am down here to inspect your recently purchased watch, if you still have it," said Richard.

"Do you have the watch here, Mr. Bourdeau?"

"No, I don't have it here," answered Bourdeau. "It's at home."

"Could you bring it in tomorrow and let me look at?" asked Richard.

"I don't have to do that, without a court order," said Bourdeau.

"I know that," responded Richard. "But a court order takes a lot of time."

After a second, he added, "You are not of any interest to us Mr. Bourdeau. We just have to check wrist watches sold during the past two weeks."

Bourdeau paused a couple of minutes and emitted a groan of annoyance. "OK," he said, "I'll bring it in tomorrow."

With that, Richard said, "Thank you Mr. Bourdeau," and left the shop.

CHAPTER 16

Richard got in his Ford Taurus and headed back to his hotel. It was about a six mile drive in the 6:00 PM after work traffic. Fresno had a population of half a million, so Richard thought it was probably in a one and a half million metropolitan area. There were several lanes of packed traffic.

The scenery and weather, however, compensated for the heavy traffic. The mountains to the east were beautiful and the weather was perfect, probably about 74°.

When he finally got back to the Holiday Inn, he went directly to his room. There were quite a few people checking into this hotel by the airport. Richard called home to tell Melanie that he arrived safely and everything was going all right.

Richard took a shower and changed his clothes. He then left his room and took the elevator to the fifth floor, where the restaurant and cocktail lounge were. Since it was about 7:00 pm, the restaurant was still crowded. Richard ordered roast duck and rice. He also ordered a good Caesar salad. The meal was very satisfying.

At about 8:30 pm, Richard strolled into the cocktail lounge. It was a fairly large room with a small bandstand on one wall. The opposite wall had a long bar with a mirror running the length of it. There must have been about twenty tables in the room, at least half of which were occupied.

Richard sat at the bar and ordered a Jack Daniels and water. Around 9:00 PM the band came out. It consisted of a girl singer and three musicians. She said good evening to everyone and said her name was Margaret. The band launched into a country music song. It was very smooth and relaxing and Margaret had a pleasant voice. Richard returned to his room about 10:30 PM. He telephoned in a wakeup call for 7:00 AM.

The next morning Richard went to the cafeteria for breakfast where he had cereal, a poached egg, orange juice, and coffee. He set out for Fresno Motors a little after 9:00 AM.

Clarence Bourdeau was in his office so Richard knocked once on the door and walked in.

Bourdeau looked up and said, "Well, I brought the watch." He opened his desk drawer and took out the watch. "It doesn't have a wristband, so I don't wear it. I intend to buy a wristband one of these days so I can wear it." He handed the watch to Richard.

Richard sat down and examined the watch. It was a gold wrist watch. On the back one could see that someone had filed a stripe across it. Richard took out his pen knife and looked at Bourdeau. "Is it all right if I open the back. I would like to see the serial number?"

Bourdeau shrugged his shoulders. "Go ahead," he said with a note of annoyance.

Richard carefully opened the watch. He set it on his lap and got out his notebook and pen. He read the many digit serial number and noted it down. He then snapped the back on the watch and handed it to Bourdeau.

"Thank you, Mr. Bourdeau," he said. "I just have to phone in the serial number. I'll use my phone in my car. Richard rose and left the office.

Back in his car, Richard took out his notebook and cell phone. He typed in the lieutenant's phone number and waited.

After a moment it was answered. "Lieutenant Adams, Seattle police," said the lieutenant.

"Hello, lieutenant, this is Hopkins. I am down here in Fresno and I have seen the watch. A Mr. Clarence Bourdeau, who lives here, bought it at a swap meet. I opened the back of the watch and got the serial number. Is Alister sitting at his desk?"

"No, I don't see him," answered the lieutenant.

"OK," responded Richard. "We have been maintaining a record of the case. Could you check our record and find a sales receipt from a watch place, Emerald City Diamond, I think. It should have the serial number written on it."

"Just a second," said the lieutenant. He put the telephone down on his desk and went to the case records. After a couple of minutes he returned.

"I found it," he said. "I'll read it out loud. Are you ready?"

"Go ahead," said Richard. "I've got my notebook and pencil ready."

The lieutenant read out the number. It matched the serial number Richard had copied from the watch.

"It matches," said Richard. "We've got the watch."

"OK," said the lieutenant. "You will have to expropriate

the watch. It is stolen property. Do you have an M-108 form with you?"

"Yes, I brought two along," answered Richard.

"All right. Inform Mr. Clarence Bourdeau that the watch is stolen property, and you have to expropriate it," said Lieutenant Adams.

"He might refuse unless I have a court order," said Richard.

"Alister can get a court order up here and fax it down if necessary," said the lieutenant.

"I'll go back in the auto repair place and speak to Clarence Bourdeau," said Richard. "I am in my car right now."

Richard shut down his phone and filled out the M-108 form. He then went back inside the auto repair company. Bourdeau was still in his office so Richard knocked and entered his office.

"Back again?" said Bourdeau.

"Yes, I have sent the serial number of your watch back to Seattle. It matches the serial number of the missing wrist watch," said Richard.

"I have often wondered what would happen if I would buy stolen property at a swap meet," said Bourdeau. "There's no way of knowing if an item at a swap meet is stolen."

"Yes, I know," said Richard. "I have an expropriation form, M-108, here. If the thief is convicted, he will be fined for the money you paid for the item and you will be reimbursed."

"Yeah, that is if the thief is convicted and has any money," said Bourdeau.

"We feel that we have a strong case," said Richard. "We have fingerprints, DNA, and serial numbers."

Richard continued, "The process of getting a conviction can take quite a lot of time. First, a Grand Jury must convene and hear the evidence from the prosecuting attorney. The Grand Jury then decides if there is probable cause to formally charge the suspect. Then the suspect must appear in court for arraignment. The suspect then goes to a pre-trial conference. At that time the judge appoints a defense attorney if the suspect does not have sufficient funds to hire an attorney. Then the judge sets a trial date. This can be several months in the future.

Bourdeau said, "How will I know how the trial is progressing?"

Richard answered, "I will give you an M-108 Expropriation Form when you give me the watch. When I turn in our portion of the M-108 form, the Seattle court system will notify you by mail of the developments and progress of the court case."

"Do you have any kind of signed receipt from the sale?" asked Richard.

"Yes," answered Bourdeau. "The person who sold it to me gave me a signed receipt."

He reached in his desk drawer and took out the sales receipt and the wristwatch. He handed them to Richard.

Richard gave him the expropriation form, M108, in exchange. Richard put the watch and receipt in his pocket and turn to leave. "We will keep you informed about the trial progress. We will inform you of the trial date. Thank you for your cooperation, Mr. Bourdeau," said Richard as he opened the door of the office to leave.

"Have you found the thief yet?" asked Bourdeau.

"We have a suspect," said Richard. "But we haven't arrested him yet."

Richard went to his car and drove back to his hotel. When he got there, he telephoned Alister at the police station in Seattle.

Alister answered on the second ring. "Alister Jensen. Seattle police."

"Hi, Alister," said Richard. "I've got the watch and sales receipt from a Mr. Clarence Bourdeau down here in Fresno California."

"The lieutenant told me about it," returned Alister. "Did Bourdeau put up any objection?"

"No, he cooperated," said Richard. "I gave him the M-108 form and told him he would be reimbursed if the thief is convicted and has money."

"Fine," responded Alister.

Richard said, "I'll start on my journey to interview Orville Svensen after lunch today."

"All right," answered Alister. "Good luck."

Richard went up to the restaurant on the fifth floor of the hotel. It was just 11:30 AM and the restaurant was starting to get busy. After waiting twenty minutes, Richard was seated in a booth. He didn't get the window table this time. The restaurant had a lot of patrons. The special was baked salmon and rice. Richard chose that, and a cup of coffee.

After lunch Richard went to his room and got out his map of Fresno. It took him about five minutes to find Hillside Avenue. The 900 block was near Wilmington Avenue. It appeared to be on the west edge of the city. He folded his map and put it in his pocket along with another

M-108 expropriation form. He left his room and took the elevator to the lobby.

When he got to his rented Ford Taurus in the parking lot he rolled down the window and drove out of the lot heading for Fresno. His hotel was about six miles from Fresno and he followed the path he had plotted on his map.

He finally arrived at Golden State Real Estate at about 2:00 PM. He walked into the establishment and went up to the girl sitting at the reception desk. The girl, whose name tag said Eldora, smiled and said, "Good afternoon. May I help you?"

Richard answered, "I would like to speak to Orville Svensen, if he is available."

Eldora looked at her computer and said, "He is out with a client, but left a note saying he expected to be back around 2:30 pm."

Richard looked around the lobby and espied an alcove with three chairs. "OK," he said, "I'll just wait for him to return. Would it be all right if I sat over there?" nodding towards the alcove.

"Certainly," answered the girl. "Would you like a cup of coffee or water?"

"Water would be fine, thank you," said Richard and walked towards the alcove. Eldora soon brought the water and Richard settle down to wait for Orville Svensen. There were several magazines to page through.

At 2:45 PM a man walked up to Richard and said, "Hello. My name is Orville Svensen. I was told that you wanted to speak to me."

Orville Svensen was about 35 years old. He had medium length blond hair. He was just under six feet in height and was of normal weight for that height. He was wearing a medium to dark blue blazer. It was the singled breasted variety with gold buttons on the front and the sleeve cuffs. He wore a light blue shirt with a conservative red tie with a geometric pattern. He had a pleasant, friendly smile and a congenial, sociable manner. Richard assumed this was the standard appearance and manner of a successful real estate agent.

Richard stood and said, "Hello, Mr. Svensen, I am detective Richard Hopkins of the Seattle Police Department. Richard showed him his badge and continued, "We are investigating a robbery in Seattle and I would just like to ask you a few questions about an item you bought recently at a swap meet."

Svensen just stared at him for a moment and then said, "OK. Would you follow me to my office."

He led Richard to an office towards the rear of the building. Svensen sat at his desk and offered Richard a chair. Svensen's office wasn't very big. It did have a window which was nice. He had a picture of his wife and two children on his desk. There was a small table pushed up against one wall. Svensen had some advertising bulletins on the table plus a small trophy he had won at playing golf.

Svensen began by saying, "So, I was at a swap meet just outside town recently and did buy something, a man's ring. It has a green emerald in a silver setting. So, why is the Seattle police department interested in it?"

Richard answered, "It might be a ring that was stolen in Seattle a couple of weeks ago. We were informed by a man who lives in Seattle and who comes down here to California to sell items at swap meets that he sold a ring to you."

Svensen said, "Well, I had no reason to think that the ring had been stolen."

"No, of course not," responded Richard. "And the man who bought it in Seattle and brought it down here to sell it didn't know it was stolen either."

"So, how do you know it was stolen?" asked Svensen.

"We have been tracking a stolen ring for some time now, and have reason to think that this is the ring," answered Richard.

"We have a good description of the ring and it will be decided in a court if the ring is the stolen one," continued Richard. "We have been tracking the stolen ring for some time now. A man, who lives in Seattle, was attacked in his home at night a couple of weeks ago. The man got into a fight with his assailant and some blood and fingerprints were deposited in the home. The police collected a lot of evidence in the house and on the entry and escape route the intruder used."

Richard continued, "After the intruder left, the victim obtained first aid at a health clinic in Seattle and then called the police. The police went to the man's home and conducted a thorough inspection of the property. The fingerprints were sent to the FBI for identification, if possible. The blood found on the premises was sent to the DNA lab to check for the identity of the intruder. A thorough search of the premises revealed that the intruder had stolen some items. One of the items was a silver ring with a green emerald inset."

"The victim had receive the ring years ago as a gift and can give a detailed description of the ring. It has several unique distinguishing marks and characteristics. During our investigation of the case we located a Seattle man who acquires secondhand goods in Seattle – at secondhand stores and garage sales - and brings them down to California to sell at swap meets. This man informed the police that he had been approached by an individual at about this time who had a silver ring with a green emerald inset that he wanted sold in a California swap meet."

"This man, who brought the ring down to California to sell it, told the Seattle police that he sold it to you. That is why we are down here talking to you."

"Well, I don't have the ring here. It is at home," said Svensen.

"Could you bring it in tomorrow, Mr. Svensen? I will give you an expropriation M-108 Form for it. If it is not the ring we're looking for, it will be returned to you."

Svensen said, "I suppose I will have to. I'll bring it in tomorrow. I will be here at 9:00 AM."

Richard said, "Thank you, Mr. Svensen. I will be here at 9:00 AM."

He stood and said, "Thank you for your time and cooperation, Mr. Orville Svensen."

Richard left the real estate office and went to his car.

CHAPTER 17

He drove back to his hotel. There were no messages for him at the desk. Richard went to his room. He kicked off his shoes and sat down in the easy chair. It was too early in the afternoon to call his wife; she might be out shopping. He'd call her around supper time.

Richard decided that he would read his notes on the case and update his records on his computer. He had brought his laptop with him. So, he spent the afternoon rereading his notes and updating his computer records.

At 5:30 PM he telephoned his wife. She answered the phone on the third ring.

Richard said, "Hi, Melanie, it's me."

Melanie responded, "Oh, hello Richard. How are things going?"

Richard answered, "I got the watch today, and I'll pick up the ring tomorrow. I contacted the man who bought the ring today. He said he would bring it to work tomorrow. He works at a real estate office."

Melanie said, "So, you will be home tomorrow night. Is that right?"

Richard answered, "Yes, I should be. How is Rachel getting along in the school band?"

Melanie said, "Oh, she loves it. She plays the flute, as you know, and her friend Jennifer plays the piccolo."

Richard said, "Well that's nice. I suppose they occasionally march while playing."

"Yes," answered Melanie, "but they usually just sit in the music studio."

"The territory around here is very attractive," said Richard. "There are mountains to the east and there's a lot of farmland once you get out of town."

"What crops do they raise down there?" asked Melanie.

"It looks like fruit orchards to me," answered Richard. "Row after row of trees and bushes planted in nice orderly rows."

"It might be citrus fruit," said Melanie, "or avocados."

"Well, I'll hang up now and let you get back to cooking supper. I suppose Rachel is home," said Richard.

"Oh, yes," answered Melanie, "she has been up in her room playing music and talking on her cell phone to her friends for hours."

"OK," said Richard. "Goodbye."

After supper in the hotel restaurant, Richard returned to his room and checked the TV schedule to see what was on. He noticed that the Dodgers were playing in Los Angeles. So, Richard turned that on and settled back to watch two hours of baseball.

Richard was up early the next morning. It was Sunday morning. He wanted to be at Orville Svensen's real estate office by 9:00 am. He didn't want to get there after nine and find that Svensen was out with a customer looking at houses for sale.

Richard had breakfast at 7:30 AM and was out on the

road driving to Svensen's real estate office before 8:30 AM. It was a six mile trip to Fresno from his hotel at the airport. It was a pleasant drive even though the highway was crowded. The weather was excellent and the scenery was absolutely beautiful.

Richard entered the real estate office just a little before 9:00 AM. The receptionist, Eldora, recognized him and offered coffee or water again. Richard sat in the visitor's alcove and had a coffee. Orville Svensen showed up at 9:05am and said "Good morning, detective. Should we go to my office?"

Richard followed Svensen to his office and took the pro-offered chair while Svensen took the ring from his briefcase.

"Here's the ring," said Svensen. "You said yesterday that you had an expropriation form to give me for it."

"Yes," said Richard. He took the form out of his pocket and handed it to Svensen.

Richard took the ring from Svensen and examined it carefully. "It certainly is a handsome ring," said Richard. He checked the band and noted that it did have the letters CMD engraved on the inside of the band.

Richard said, "If this is not the stolen ring, then it will be returned to you."

Svensen said, "If it is stolen property, will I be reimbursed some way, or am I just out the money?" Svensen handed Richard a receipt and said, "I received this receipt at the swap meet when I bought it. I paid $325 for it."

Richard responded, "The court will fine the culprit if he is convicted for the full amount. The court will then reimburse you."

Svensen asked, "If your suspect is not convicted then I get the ring back, right?"

Richard answered, "Yes, if he is not convicted we will return your ring by insured postal delivery."

"How long will all this take?" asked Svensen. "Will the court case occur in a month or will it take longer?"

Richard answered, "It usually takes longer. The prosecuting attorney will have to file charges and then the case will have to be put on the docket."

Richard continued, "First, we apprehend our suspect. A Grand Jury must then meet and hear the evidence from the prosecuting attorney and then decide if there is probable cause to formally charge the suspect. Then the suspect must appear in court for arraignment. At that time the judge assigns a defense attorney for the suspect if the suspect requests one. The judge then sets the trial date. That date can be a month or more in the future.

"Since we have expropriated the ring, Mr. Svensen, and given you an M-108 Form for it, the Seattle court will send you a successions of letters informing you of the progress of the case."

"So, it might take several months," said Svensen. "Is that it?"

"Yes, probably," answered Richard.

"How will I know how it is progressing?" asked Svensen.

"The Seattle court system will keep you posted, now that I am taking possession," answered Richard.

"OK," said Svensen.

Richard put the ring in a briefcase he had brought along with him and turned towards the door. "Thank you for your cooperation, Mr. Svensen," he said and left Svensen's office.

Richard had noticed a Lutheran Church in Fresno on his way to the real estate office and decided to attend the service there before returning to his room at the airport.

After the church service, Richard drove back to his hotel at the airport and packed his suit case. His airline ticket indicated a 3:30pm flight. He checked out of his hotel room and drove to the automobile rental site. He returned the car and took the shuttle to the air terminal.

Richard preferred to get to the airport and get checked in and then have lunch at the airport restaurant. He knew that if he had lunch at an outside restaurant and then drove to the airport, he wouldn't be able to relax.

Richard found the airport restaurant on the second floor. He had two and one half hours before his plane took off. He figured he would leave the restaurant and get in the check in line at least an hour before take-off time.

The restaurant was spacious and had a huge window overlooking the airplane runways. The waitress led him to a table where he had an unobstructed view of the landing field. She handed him a menu and filled his water glass. Richard ordered a pork chop, well done, and fried potatoes and broccoli.

Richard gazed out the window at the airfield. A 777 was just taxiing to the take-off position. Richard always thought that the 777 was a graceful, well-proportioned airplane. After a minute the airplane revved up its engines and roared down the runway.

A few single engine airplanes used an auxiliary landing strip a few hundred yards away. A military jet flew over at one point. At 2:00 PM Richard paid his bill and left the restaurant. He had one and a half hours before his flight took off.

Richard went through the lengthy, hour-long process of being checked in. He knew the careful inspection of passengers was necessary.

Richard's airplane landed right on schedule at SeaTac airport in Seattle. Melanie and Rachel were at SeaTac when Richard emerged from the check in line. They were home in time for supper. Melanie made chili that night. It had been on slow simmer while they were at the airport.

The next day, Richard turned in the wristwatch and emerald ring to the property department at the police station. It was Monday, September 26th, eleven days after the robbery. He then went to his cubicle in the squad room.

"Congratulations on your detective work in retrieving the stolen watch and ring from California, Richard," said Alister.

"Thank you," responded Richard.

"Yes, finding out about Stone and Atinsky's business deals for selling merchandise in California really solved this case for us," said Alister.

"Yeah, we heard about Atinsky from our interview with Stone," said Richard. "Remember how he said he acquired some of his statues and pottery from Atinsky."

"On a subsequent interview with Atinsky," said Richard, "I learned that he'd received a watch and ring from Stone to sell in those California swap meets."

Alister said, "Fortunately, we had the serial number of the watch and knew about the engraving on the ring to identify them."

"Right," said Richard.

"All our footwork going to those pawn shops on First Avenue, downtown, and the airport turned up nothing," said Alister.

Richard laughed. "This time it turned out that way."

"While you were in California retrieving the watch and ring I went over the case with forensics. I wanted to make sure that we didn't jump to the conclusion that Stone was the culprit after examining too little evidence," said Alister.

"I know you mentioned several times that DuBois claimed to have seen the intruder carrying a bag," said Richard. "However, we only have Stone in possession of a watch and ring."

"Yes," responded Alister. "I suppose it is possible that Stone came with a bag and just didn't want to leave it behind."

"Yeah, that would be incriminating evidence," said Richard.

"Anyway, I decided to go over all our evidence with Ralph Lee down at the forensics building on Rainier Avenue," said Alister. "Ralph has all our blood samples and finger prints from the case. And, then I went to check with James Newton in forensics on the fifth floor of the police station."

"So, you went to check with both of them. That would be the right way to do it," said Richard.

"I went to see Newton the next day," answered Alister. "Newton and his assistants were the people who showed up at DuBois' apartment when we first responded to the crime."

"Did you and Ralph Lee or Newton turn up any additional evidence or any new leads to follow?" asked Richard.

"No, James Newton and I talked about the blood drops on the floor in DuBois' apartment and bathroom," said Alister.

"The blood drops that Stone said he dropped when he cut his hand on the coffee cup," put in Richard.

"Right," said Alister. "But James Newton said he found no others."

"Did James detect any finger prints on the bookend that was used to strike DuBois?" asked Richard.

"No, whoever wielded the bookend wore gloves," answered Alister.

"Did James Newton suggest any new leads?" asked Richard.

"No, there were several finger prints on the bureau that was tipped over. But DuBois had numerous visitors over time."

"Did Newton check the window sill where the intruder entered and left?" asked Richard.

"Yes," answered Alister. "Newton said there were smudges, not finger prints, on the window and window sill. The intruder wore gloves. Newton did emphasized that the intruder apparently tore his glove going down the fire escape and left a bloody fingerprint."

"Did Newton discover anything new and suggest any new leads to follow out?" asked Richard.

"No," answered Alister. "He spoke to DuBois several days after the crime. He asked DuBois to examine that bureau again to see if anything was missing besides the watch and ring. DuBois complied and told Newton later that nothing else was missing."

"So, the next day you visited with Ralph Lee in the forensics lab on Rainier Avenue," continued Richard.

"Yes, answered Alister. We went over all the evidence again on the bandages that I gave him from the 24 hour clinic on Pine Street that DuBois went to. Ralph Lee sent the bandages with blood spots to the FBI in Washington for DNA analysis but hasn't heard back yet."

"So, it seems that we have covered everything," said Richard. "We haven't missed anything."

The lieutenant had scheduled a meeting in his office at 10:00 AM for Alister and Richard. The lieutenant opened the meeting with, "Let's review where we are on this case. Alister, why don't you start."

Alister began, "Richard brought back the wrist watch and emerald ring from California."

The lieutenant said, "Well, that's solid progress."

Alister continued, "I've telephoned Caspar DuBois and asked him to come down here and identify the ring, if he can. He said he would be here tomorrow."

Richard put in, "The description Dubois gave us of the ring two weeks ago certainly matches the ring I turned in to the property department this morning."

Alister said, "And we know that we have the correct wristwatch because the serial number inside the watch matches the serial number on the watch sales receipt that Dubois has."

The lieutenant said, "So, let's say that we have recovered the stolen property. Atinsky says he got them from Siegfried Stone and sold them to the two people Richard spoke to in California."

The lieutenant continued, "The weak point in the case is

that Stone can claim that he found them in the grass along the sidewalk in Dubois' neighborhood. And, we can not prove otherwise."

"Right," said Alister, "So our strongest piece of evidence is Stone's bloody fingerprint on the fire escape outside Dubois' room."

"It is actually difficult to prove things," said Alister. "Stone was slick enough to deposit some of his own blood in Caspar DuBois' apartment before the crime by cutting his finger while visiting with Dubois."

"Right," put in the lieutenant. "It would be very difficult to prove that a drop of Stone's blood found by the forensic team after the crime was deposited during the crime and not before the crime."

"The only way to do that," said Alister, "would be to prove that the drop of blood was lying on a piece of furniture that was not in the room on the day Stone cut his finger. Then the drop would have had to fall on the day of the robbery."

"Stone's claim that he found the watch and ring in the grass outside Dubois' apartment is a similar thing," said Richard. "How can you prove that he took them from Dubois' room and not found them on the grass?"

"You would need a camera in Dubois' apartment that took a picture of Stone removing the watch and ring from Dubois' bureau," said the lieutenant.

"Fortunately, we have the fire escape bracket with Stone's bloody fingerprint and Dubois' blood commingled on the bracket," said Richard.

"Correct," said the lieutenant.

"Yes, things are very difficult to prove in a case," said Alister again.

"Well, maybe that will be sufficient in court," said the lieutenant. The meeting broke up at that point.

Alister and Richard sat at their desks at police headquarters the next afternoon.

In the middle of the afternoon, Alister received a phone call informing him that Caspar DuBois was at the front desk and asking for him. When Alister got to the front desk, he said to Caspar DuBois, "Hello, Mr. Dubois. Have you come to identify the ring?"

"Yes," answered Dubois.

"OK, Mr. Dubois. Let's go to the Recovered Property department and view the ring that Richard Hopkins brought back from California."

When they got there, Alister presented the property receipt form to the attendant at the desk. When she brought up the ring, Caspar DuBois, with a joyous grin on his face, readily identified the ring as his. "It's mine all right," said Dubois. "This inscription on the inside of the ring band is my initials."

"All right, Mr. Dubois," said Alister, "you won't be able to take possession of it until after the trial."

"OK," answered Dubois.

Alister took a legal attest form from his pocket and put it on the counter. "I would like for you to sign this attest form that asserts that this ring is yours."

Caspar DuBois filled out the form and signed it.

Alister escorted Caspar DuBois to the police department lobby, and then he returned to his cubicle.

"We have made some progress in the case so far," said

Richard. "We have found the stolen goods: wrist watch and silver ring with green emerald inset."

"Right," responded Alister. "That's always an achievement in a robbery case. But can we use it to get a conviction?"

"The identification of Siegfried Stone as the person who gave the watch to Edward Atinsky is fairly strong," said Richard. "Atinsky's testimony in court might be effective."

"Let's both go over to the REI store on Denny Avenue this afternoon with Stone's photographed," said Alister.

"All right," said Richard. I'll write my report on the trip to Fresno, California tomorrow."

Alister reached for his jacket and they headed for the door. They took the elevator down to the garage and requested an unmarked detective car. They were given a gray Toyota. Richard drove to the REI on Denny. Richard drove into their parking lot but couldn't find a vacant slot. He then drove out of the parking lot and circled the block twice. Again, he couldn't find a vacant parking place. He finally parked in the parking lot of a restaurant a block away.

CHAPTER 18

When Alister entered the REI store, he marveled again at how much camping equipment they had to sell. Alister didn't do much camping and wasn't greatly interested in their equipment.

He did admire some of the tents. They had a large and diverse supply of cooking utensils.

Alister looked for the manager who had given Newton from the forensics department the samples of cloth. They went up to one of the clerks and asked her where the manager's office was. She pointed to a staircase and said the manager's office was on the second floor. Richard and Alister took the stairs and found a door with a plaque on the side saying manager.

Alister knocked on the door and waited. He soon heard someone within the office say come in. They entered. The room was quite spacious with a large desk in the middle. The man seated behind the desk was about 45 years old and dressed in a suit. The suit seemed a little strange for a sporting goods store that sold equipment to hikers. There were numerous photographs on the walls taken from various scenic perspectives in the mountains.

"Hello," said Alister. "I am detective Alister Jensen of

the Seattle police department. And, this is Richard Hopkins of the detective department." He displayed his badge.

"How do you do, detectives," answered the manager. "My name is Alexander Brown. How can I help?"

"Mr. Brown, our forensics investigator, James Newton, was here a few days ago to check on some skiing or hiking parkas that are involved in a case we are processing."

"Yes, I recall," said Mr. Brown.

"One of your tailors gave Mr. Newton some samples or strips of cloth from a parka you sell," said Alister.

"That's correct," said Brown. "I directed one of our tailors to do that. Did it help?"

"Yes," answered Alister. "Our forensics lab was able to ascertain that some scraps of cloth found at the crime scene matched the type of cloth you provided."

"Good," said Brown. "I am glad we could help."

"Do you sell many parkas of that type, Mr. Brown?" asked Alister.

"Not too many at this time of the year. Maybe, ten or so parkas per months in August," answered Brown.

"Mr. Brown, I wonder if I could show some photographs of possible customers to those members of your sales staff who sold parkas recently," said Alister.

"Just a moment," said Brown. "I'll check my computer for the sales slip records of parkas."

He consulted his computer for a few minutes and said, "We sold eight black parkas between June 1 and August 30. They were sold by one woman on our staff, Jody McDermott. She works in that department."

"Would it be possible for me to interview her?" asked Alister.

"Yes, I think so," answered Brown. "I'll go down stairs and ask her to come up here."

Brown stood and said, "There is a room at the end of the hall on this floor with the sign 'Conference Room' on the door. If you wait in there I'll bring Jody McDermott up."

Alister and Richard proceeded down the hall to the room marked 'Conference Room' while Brown went downstairs.

Alister opened a briefcase he had been carrying and took out a folder containing photographs. The folder contained photos of Caspar DuBois, Siegfried Stone, Edward Atinsky, and several Seattle police officers. Alister also took out of his briefcase a foldable easel. He opened the easel and set it up on a table in the room.

Alister knew that when he would place one photographs at a time on the easel, Jody would be looking straight ahead at the photo and he and Richard would get a good view of Jody's facial expression. If he placed each photo one at time on a table, Jody would be looking down and Richard and he would not see her facial expression as well.

Alister and Richard also positioned themselves around the table in such a manner as to see Jody's facial expressions clearly.

About five minutes later, Brown and a young woman entered the room.

"Jody," said Brown, "these men are detective Alister Jensen and detective Richard Hopkins of the Seattle police department. They have some questions about our sale of the black ski parkas last summer."

Alister showed Jody his badge and said, "Good afternoon, Jody. We are investigating a robbery and a black ski parka has come up in connection with the robbery. I would like to show you some photographs and ask if you can identify one of the people as a customer who bought a black parka this last summer."

Alexander Brown smiled and left the room.

Jody said, "What black parka? I sell a lot of parkas."

She was obviously upset and apprehensive. Alister thought that a lot of people are apprehensive and frightened when confronted by the police department.

Alister said, "A certain black parka was involved in the commission of a robbery. The parka is like those sold here."

Jody looked at him wide-eyed and obviously frightened.

Alister continued, "We would just like you to look at some photographs and tell me if any of the men look like someone you sold a black parka to in the past few months."

"Will I have to testify in court?" asked Jody in a terrified voice.

"Maybe, Jody, but not necessarily," answered Alister.

Alister began placing the photographs, one at a time, on the easel and Jody watched intently. When Alister placed Siegfried Stone's photograph on the easel, Jody made a slight start and move forward and peered carefully at the photo.

Jody said, "I think I saw this man in here, but I might have just seen him on the street."

Alister continued to place the other photos on the easel. When Alister had finished placing all photos on the easel he took the easel down and thanked Jody for her time and assistance.

Alister and Richard were quite sure that Jody thought she recognized Siegfried Stone.

"Does the hood come attached to the parka?" asked Richard. "I suppose you can detach it if you want."

"Yes, this model comes with detachable hood," said Jody.

"I am recalling things a little better now," said Jody. "I think I did sell the parka to this man in the photograph." She paused, and then added defensively, "But I am not sure."

"Do you recall about when he bought it, or if he paid in cash or used a credit card?" asked Richard.

Jody paused a minute to recollect. "I think it was the third week of August," she said. "As I recall," she continued, "he paid in cash."

Alister and Richard glanced at each other and Alister said, "Well, thank you for helping us, Jody. We will be leaving now."

He took a card from his coat and handed it to her. "Here is my card, Jody. If you think of anything else later, please don't hesitate to telephone me."

Alister and Richard turned and left the room. When they got back in their car and headed for the station, Alister said, "That gives us some more evidence against Siegfried Stone but I don't know how well it will stand up in court."

"Yes," returned Richard, "a good defense lawyer could weaken it in front of the jury. She wasn't absolutely convinced that she recognized Stone."

"And those black parkas might be sold in a lot of sports stores in the country," put in Alister.

They drove in silence the rest of the way back to the station.

When they got back to their cubicle in the squad room, Alister said, "I think I'll come in tomorrow and type up my report, as far as we've gotten. There doesn't seem to be much else to do until the FBI report on the blood or DNA and fingerprints comes in."

"Right," said Richard. "I agree." After a pause, he continued, "You don't think we have seized on a suspect too soon and ignored other leads, do you?"

"I don't think so," answered Alister. "I suppose we could go over the forensics report again tomorrow and see if there are any leads we ignored because we were so convinced that Siegfried Stone was our man. But, as I told you before I went over the forensic data with both Ralph Lee and James Newton while you were in California and we couldn't find anything new."

At that point Richard's phone rang. When he answered, Ralph Lee told him that he had a fingerprint report for him.

When Richard got to Ralph Lee's office, Ralph was at his desk. Richard knocked once and went in. "Good afternoon, Ralph," he said, "I have come to see the fingerprint report you have for me."

"Hi, Richard," said Ralph Lee. "Come on in and sit down." He reached for a report in a basket on his desk.

Ralph handed the report to Richard. "This FBI report came in last night," Ralph said. "They identified the fingerprint on that wrist watch as that of Siegfried Stone. Remember I told you a few days ago that the FBI had a record on Stone from some arrests and convictions in other states over the past 10 years."

"Yes, I recall," said Richard, paging through the report. "A fingerprint on it might not help us much. Stone told us that he had visited Caspar DuBois in the past. So his fingerprint on the wrist watch might not help us."

"I guess you're right," said Ralph.

"Did you discover anything else from the watch when you examined it?" asked Richard.

"It was wiped clean except for some partial fingerprints on it," replied Ralph.

"How about the silver ring with green emerald inset?" asked Richard. "Did the FBI find fingerprints on that?"

"Yes," answered Ralph. He handed another paper to Richard. "They found Siegfried Stone's fingerprints on that also."

"We probably won't be able to use the ring or watch fingerprint evidence in the court room because Stone will just say that he had visited Caspar DuBois many times in his apartment and at Arnold's Broiler," said Richard.

"You would think that Stone would have wiped both the watch and the ring carefully before giving them to Atinsky to sell in a California swap meet," continued Richard.

"He probably did," responded Ralph. "But when he handed them to Atinsky, Stone would not want to be wearing gloves. That would appear too suspicions and Atinsky would think that the items were stolen."

"So, Stone would have wiped them clean and then only touched them in one or two small places while handing them to Atinsky," said Richard.

"Yes, probably," answered Ralph.

"Well, I'm glad we found both stolen articles and determined who stole them even if we can't use the evidence in a courtroom," said Richard.

Richard thanked Ralph for his help and took the FBI reports that Ralph had handed him. He then returned to his cubicle in the detective squad room.

When Alister got home, he left his shoes at the door

and went through the living room to the patio glass door. He opened the glass door and stepped out onto the patio. Beautiful day again he thought. Maybe it is clouding up a little but there is still a magnificent view of the mountains. He went to the kitchen to get a beer from the refrigerator. On his way back to the patio he stopped at his music table, selected a disc, and put it on. Out on the patio his thoughts turned to what he should fix for supper.

When Alister arrived at the office the next morning, Richard was already in the cubicle.

"Greetings," said Alister when he entered.

"Hi, Alister," responded Richard. "I got the forensic report from the records office on the third floor."

"OK," said Alister. "Let me get a cup of coffee first."

Alister hung up his jacket and left the cubicle. He took the elevator to the first floor. Margaret was at the Randolphs counter and there weren't too many people in line.

When Alister's turn came up at the counter, Margaret said, "The usual?"

Alister answered, "Yes, single shot Americano."

Alister glanced at the headlines on the newspaper as he walked towards the elevator, coffee cup in hand. The headlines reported another shooting of police officers, this time in Denver.

When he got back to his cubicle on the third floor, Richard was sitting back in his chair with the forensics report in his hands and his feet on his desk.

Richard looked over and said, "There isn't much to the forensics report. The intruder apparently wore surgical gloves because there aren't any finger prints in the expected places."

"Did they find any fragments of anything other than the few torn black parka cloth pieces?" asked Alister.

"No," said Richard. "They think they found where the intruder was standing when Dubois socked him. They decided that from some scuff marks on the floor and a knocked over lamp. But nothing fell from him on that occasion."

"I think our intruder was smart enough to not bring anything he could drop," said Alister. "He only brought what he needed. He knew Caspar DuBois didn't have a gun."

"The investigators have decided where the intruder and victim were standing when Dubois was hit with the bookend," went on Richard. "The scuff marks on the rug and Dubois' fingerprints on a shelf and ashtray on the floor indicate where Dubois took his fall."

"Does the report say anything about the scuff marks you allude to?" asked Alister.

"It says they examined the scuff marks and the guy's shoes were on the tarmac in the alley behind the building where Dubois lives and also on some pavement where there was a lot of a certain chemical they mention here," answered Richard. "It says this chemical is present in the soap solution used by construction and repair companies after they do their work."

"I suppose they checked on construction and repairs in the city," put in Alister.

"Oh, yes," said Richard. "And guess what? Four construction companies did work recently in the city and one of them repaired a leaking city drainpipe in the parking lot behind Siegfried Stone's apartment."

"One thing that I have wondered about from the start,"

said Alister, "is that Dubois said he noticed the intruder carrying a bag or pillowcase. Yet, Dubois reported only a watch and a ring missing."

"Maybe, the intruder's movements woke Dubois up early," said Alister. "Perhaps the intruder didn't get all he came for."

"That's basically all there is in the forensic report. There's the talk about the blood drops. But we know that. And, also, Siegfried Stone's statement about cutting his finger a few days before the robbery," said Richard, putting the forensic report down.

Richard continued, "I went to Ralph Lee's lab yesterday following his phone call to me."

"What did he have to say?" asked Alister.

"He had received back the report from the FBI on the watch and ring I brought back from California," said Richard.

"What had they discovered?" asked Alister.

"The FBI found Stone's fingerprints on both the watch and the ring," answered Richard.

Alister said, "Stone must not have wiped them very clean."

"Ralph and I figure that Stone probably had wiped them clean but he had to touch them when he handed them to Atinsky," said Richard. "It would have appeared too suspicious to Atinsky if Stone had been wearing gloves."

"Yeah, probably," responded Alister.

"So, again," said Richard, "Stone's lawyer will just say Stone's fingerprints are on the watch and ring because he visited Dubois at his apartment occasionally."

"Yes," responded Alister. "At least we have recovered the stolen goods."

"Right," said Richard. "It wasn't all a waste of time and money for me to go down to California."

Richard continued, "The really strong thing here in the forensics report is the bloody fingerprint on the fire escape bracket."

"Yes, I think that is what we will use effectively in the court room," said Alister.

"It doesn't look like there are any leads or evidence that we missed, or failed to follow up on," said Richard.

"No," returned Alister. "No one will be able to accuse us of selecting a suspect early on and ignoring other evidence."

Chapter 19

At that moment, the lieutenant came striding over. "Well, detectives," he said, "the DNA and fingerprint report from the FBI just came in. It is down in the secure transmission room."

"Great," said Alister, "we will go get it."

Alister and Richard went downstairs to the secure transmission room on the second floor. The secure transmissions room sends and receives messages that are encoded at the originating site and then sent either by high frequency radio or by satellite to the destination site. The message is then decoded at the destination site.

Alister and Richard went up to the counter in the secure communication room. Charlotte was working the station and said, "Good morning, Alister. Nice to see you."

Alister answered, "Hi, Charlotte, how are you today?"

"Fine," she answered. "What can I do for you gentlemen today?"

"Our lieutenant just informed us that a message has arrived for us from Washington," said Alister.

Charlotte said, "Just a moment," and went into the room behind her desk.

When she came back, she placed a sealed envelope on

the counter and a receipt for Alister to sign. Alister signed the receipt and picked up the envelope. "Thanks, Charlotte," he said as he and Richard left the room.

Alister and Richard went back directly to their office before opening the envelope. One was not supposed to open mail received in the secure transmission room unless you were in your office or cubicle.

When they arrived in their cubicle, Alister opened the envelope. He read the report and spoke to Richard. "The fingerprint found on the fire escape is that of Siegfried Stone. They had a fingerprint record of him from a case in Illinois."

"Yeah, that's what we figured," said Richard.

Alister went on, "DNA analysis of the blood found in the fingerprint indicates blood from two different people. One person was Siegfried Stone again."

"That's probably due to the cut on his cheek and lip where Dubois hit him," said Richard.

"The second person's blood and DNA," went on Alister, "matched the DNA from the sample of blood we took from Dubois and mailed along with our request to the FBI."

"OK," exclaimed Richard. "That clinches it. Stone's fingerprint on the fire escape has his blood and Dubois' blood on it."

"Yes," responded Alister. "There is more. The drops of blood the forensic team found on the floor and furniture also has the DNA of Stone and Dubois."

Alister handed the envelope and report to Richard so he could read it. Alister said, "I think it is time for us to confer with the lieutenant and then assemble and write up our case."

"Then we can make an appointment at the prosecuting attorney's office to present our case to him," said Richard.

"Right," said Alister.

They looked over at the lieutenant's office to see if he was busy.

"Nobody is talking to the lieutenant, now," said Alister. "Let's go over."

"OK," said Richard. They went over to Lieutenant Adam's office. Richard took along the envelope and report from the FBI. He knocked on the lieutenant's door and waited.

"Come on in," said the lieutenant. "Did you get the blood and fingerprint report from the FBI?"

"Yes," said Richard as they entered. "I have it here."

"It confirms everything we expected," said Alister.

The three men and sat down and discussed the entire case.

Alister said, "I keep thinking about the remark that Dubois made about seeing his assailant carrying a bag or pillowcase around during the night of the break-in. Yet, we are saying he only took a watch and a ring."

"Do you think we should get a search warrant and search his apartment?" asked Richard.

"Yes," answered Alister. "There might be something we will need at the trial, or maybe we could find more stolen property."

The lieutenant said, "Alister, go to the court house and get a search warrant. We should be sure of our case."

"I think we are ready to present the case to the prosecuting attorney," said Lieutenant Adams. "You two write up the case carefully and make an appointment at the prosecuting attorney's office to present it."

"All right, we will," said Alister. Alister and Richard stood and left the lieutenant's office. They went back to their cubicle and got out all the reports and information that they had previously written and typed. They turned their desks to face each other. Richard was a good and fast typist. So, he would type as they both went over their papers and assembled their case in a coherent manner. They had typed up their previous cases this way, and it had worked fine.

When they were done three hours later they had a twenty page report with fifteen attachments.

"I think it's complete and adequate," said Richard.

"Yeah, it's not bad," said Alister.

Alister looked at the clock. "4:15," he said. "It's early enough to call the prosecutor's office and make an appointment. Let's see, today is Wednesday, September 28."

He picked up his phone, consulted his list of phone numbers, and dialed. After talking for a few minutes he hung up and announced, "Our appointment is 9:00 AM, Friday."

On his way home from his office, Alister thought it would be nice to go over to the peninsula some Saturday. The weather was great. He could call Denise and maybe they could go some Saturday soon. They could stay at Forks and go down from there either to the beach on the Pacific or for a hike in the rain forest. Denise was a computer programmer and worked five days a week. Maybe they could just go out for supper at some restaurant tomorrow, Thursday.

At 7:00 PM, Alister telephoned Denise.

"Hello," answered Denise after three rings.

"Hi, Denise, it's Alister," he said. "How are you today?"

"Oh, Alister," she said. "Hi. You usually call on Fridays. Anything new happening?"

"Richard and I just finished a case," answered Alister. "All we have to do tomorrow is conduct a search warrant. I was just wondering if you would like to go to supper tomorrow night."

"OK," said Denise. "I should be home at six as usual."

"We could go to that Italian restaurant in Seattle," said Alister. "The one that serves meals by bringing serving dishes to your table rather than individual servings on plates."

"Oh, yes, I like that place," said Denise. "Their food tastes so good."

"OK," answered Alister. "I'll pick you up at 6:30 PM, then,"

"All right, I'll see you then," said Denise.

They said goodbye and hung up.

Alister went out to his kitchen and after examining his refrigerator contents he decided to have grilled salmon. He decided that after supper he would read a mystery.

Early the next morning, Thursday, Alister went to the court house to request a search warrant from the presiding judge. He used the FBI report on the fingerprints and DNA to convince the judge that Stone was probably DuBois' assailant.

By 10 AM, Alister and Richard were at Stone's apartment. Richard said to Alister, "If he is home, we will just walk in and show him our search warrant. We will tell him stand aside while we conduct our search. And, if he is not home, we will get an entrance key from the manager."

Alister agreed, "Yes, that will work."

They knocked on Stone's door and got no answer. Alister went down to the manager's apartment and got the key.

"OK, let's take a look at his apartment," Alister said.

They entered Stone's apartment. Stone's clothes were strewn about the place.

"I guess he doesn't straighten up his apartment before he leaves," said Richard.

"Apparently not", responded Alister.

Alister said, "Why don't you check the bathroom and bedroom. I'll check the kitchen and living room."

Alister looked on shelves and opened drawers and looked for anything that could serve as evidence of Stone having been in DuBois's apartment.

After about 15 minutes, Richard looked in and said, "I have found nothing that looks like it might be DuBois' property."

"No, I haven't either. Evidently Stone brought an empty pillow case back from DuBois's apartment to his apartment after the robbery. The scuffle in DuBois' apartment precluded any attempt to get anything more than the watch and ring"

Richard and Alister decided to leave Stone's apartment and return to the police station.

When they got to their cubicle they wrote up their report on the search warrant. They concluded that Stone probably got nothing more than the watch and ring due to the fight in DuBois' apartment. Alister decided in the afternoon to go home and get ready for his date with Denise.

She was ready on time and as usual Alister was a little late. They went to the Italian restaurant and had to wait in line about ten minutes. The restaurant always had a line; it was very popular. When they were seated, Alister ordered lasagna. Denice ordered a veal dish. The food was served on platters so they each got some of both dishes.

After a while, Alister asked, "So, what are you working on now?"

"We are working on Vista 16," said Denise. "We've been at it for over a year now."

"Is that another operating system?" asked Alister.

"Yes," answered Denice. It's an extension and improvement over Vista 15."

"I took one course in operating systems in the computer science department of the university," said Alister. "I think we studied some simple model of an operating system devised by the computer science department of one of the universities in the Midwest that our professor found in a manual for college teachers."

"I've heard of it," said Denise.

"The operating system is only a few hundred lines long," said Alister. "Just enough to present all the required operations."

"The one I'm working on at Vista," said Denice, "is way over a million lines long."

"I don't see how you can even comprehend such a huge kludge," said Alister. "How can you keep anything straight?"

"I just visualize it as a number of sections or boxes, each doing its thing," answered Denise with a smile.

When they were done at the restaurant they went for a short walk partway around the block before going home. It was a well lighted and safe neighborhood. There were quite a few stores and filling stations and such that were open.

Alister got to work at 7:30 AM, Friday, September 30th. Richard came in a few minutes later.

"Hi, Alister," said Richard when he entered the cubicle.

"Today is our big day," said Alister. "We have to convince the prosecutor that we have a winnable case, and not just a lot of suspicions and circumstantial evidence."

"Right," responded Richard.

They gathered all their documents and evidence records together and placed them in Alister's briefcase. They then sat down, took a deep breath, and relaxed. They had forty minutes before their appointment.

"We present our case to the city's prosecuting attorney, Mark Jefferson," said Alister. "He will probably have one of his assistant prosecutors along to hear our presentation."

"Do you think Mark will present the case in court?" asked Richard.

"No, I doubt it," answered Alister. "He usually prosecutes only newsworthy or celebrity cases in court. He lets his assistants prosecute lesser cases."

"Yeah, I suppose," responded Richard.

"The prosecutor he has along for our presentation might be the one he assigns," said Alister.

"I see you have on your best suit and tie for the occasion," said Richard.

"It is not my best suit, but it is new," said Alister.

"Well it is not a formal suit," said Richard. "But it has a very nice informal herringbone jacket."

"Yes," answered Alister. "I got it at Alderwood Mall. What do you think of the tie? It took quite a while to select it. I went to three stores."

"It's a very attractive shade of blue," answered Richard. "It's a knit tie isn't it. I haven't seen a plain knit tie in a while."

"Yes, it is knit," said Alister. "I haven't seen knit ties either for quite a while. But I thought it looked great."

Richard smoothed the front of his sport coat. "I wore my dark blue sport coat this morning. My wife said I looked casually dressed, but elegant."

With that, Alister looked at his watch and said "Its 8:30 am, let's get going."

CHAPTER 20

It was only a four block walk from the police station to the municipal court. They entered the first floor lobby from Second Avenue. It was bright and pleasant since the sun was out brightly and the ceiling glass roof, three stories up, had many colors of glass in it. Alister had to open his briefcase to show the officers at the entry gate to the building that he had only papers in his case. They proceeded to the bank of elevators and went up to the third floor.

They proceeded down the hall to the prosecuting attorney's suite of offices. They entered the office complex and went up to one of the girls sitting at the reception counter.

Alister said, "We have an appointment with the prosecutor at 9:00 AM. I am Alister Jensen." He showed her his badge.

The girl looked at his badge and consulted her computer for a moment. She said, "If you would take a seat over there," nodding to a group of chairs, "someone will be out momentarily."

Alister and Richard did as directed. After about ten minutes, a girl came up to them from the hall behind the reception counter and said, "Please follow me."

She led them to a room down the hall, knocked once, ushered them into a room containing a large desk, several easy chairs, and numerous books on shelves lining the walls. Two people besides their guide were in the room.

The man behind the desk stood and said, "Good morning detectives Jensen and Hopkins. I am prosecuting attorney Mark Jefferson and this is attorney Alfreda Jones of the prosecutor's office. Please be seated."

The girl who had ushered them down the hall took a seat behind a computer.

Alister and Richard said good morning and sat down.

Mark Jefferson picked up a sheaf of papers from his desk and began, "It is nice to see you again, Alister Jensen. It has been over a year since we last met. It was the Greenbaum case as I recall."

"Yes, it was, sir," answered Alister.

"This time, it is a robbery case and the victim is Caspar DuBois," said the prosecutor glancing at his papers.

"Yes," answered Alister. He reached into his briefcase and pulled out the collection of records that he and Richard had amassed in the case; their analysis was on top. "If I might," he said, reaching the papers forward to the prosecutor's desk.

The prosecutor picked them up and leafed through them. "So, tell us about your case, detective Jensen," he said.

Alister began, "Mr. Caspar DuBois was attacked, during the night of September 15[th,] at his apartment at 1204 Third avenue, apartment 205. The thief stole a wristwatch and a silver ring with a green emerald inset. He woke up Caspar DuBois, possibly by rustling some papers or closing a bureau drawer. A fight ensued. Mr. Dubois was struck on his chin, probably by a book end, and fell to the floor. The thief departed through a window that has a fire escape leading to the alley behind the building."

"Does the victim claim that he saw and can identify the intruder?" asked the prosecutor.

"No, Mr. Dubois said his attacker wore a mask," answered Alister.

"Did you recovered the stolen property?" asked the prosecutor.

"Yes, we did," answered Alister.

"Your report, here," said the prosecutor, "says you have a suspect. A Mr. Siegfried Stone."

"Yes, we do, although we haven't arrested him yet," returned Alister.

"Please outline your case for us, Mr. Jensen," said the prosecutor.

Alister began, "A telephone call to 911 was placed at 7:00 AM, September 15. Richard and I were next up at the detective squad room at the station, and so we were assigned the case. It was a robbery with assault. We went to the address provided by the caller. His name and address are Caspar DuBois, 1204 Third Avenue, apartment 205. When we got there the responding police officer, who had that district, was already on the premises. Caspar DuBois was present. He had a bandage on the side of his jaw."

Jefferson interrupted, "Did he say that he put the bandage on by himself while waiting for the police to arrive?"

"No," answered Richard, "He went to the 24 hour medical clinic on Fourth Avenue and Pine Street before making his 911 call."

"Apparently, he figured the injury he sustained in the

robbery was more important than the property he lost in the robbery," said Alister.

Alister continued his narrative, "Dubois' apartment showed signs of a scuffle or fight. I asked Dubois to tell us what had happened and how he got his bandaged wound. He told us that he was awakened about 1:00 AM by some sound or a nudge to his bed and looked around to discover that an intruder was in his apartment. I asked him what he did upon discovering the intruder."

Dubois told us that he shouted, "Who are you?" Dubois said he couldn't identify him because he was wearing a mask or ski cap. Dubois said the man lunged at him and struck a glancing blow to his shoulder. Dubois then said the fight began and that he called out for help once. Dubois said that he landed one good solid blow on the intruder's cheek and knocked him to the floor. But the fight resumed and the intruder eventually struck Dubois on his left jaw and knocked him down. This enabled the intruder to grasp a bag off the floor and climb out the window. There is a fire escape just outside the window and the intruder escaped that way. Dubois said the intruder ran out of the alley and turned up the street. That would be Stewart Street. He didn't use an automobile.

Jefferson asked, "Did Dubois give pursuit?"

"No, apparently not," said Richard. "He was more concerned about his bleeding jaw and missing property."

Alister continued, "Richard and I checked Dubois' room to see if the intruder dropped anything in the fight. We couldn't spot anything, except maybe a black button, which we entered into the record as possible evidence."

Richard said, "We found a book end lying on the floor

with some blood on it. We figure the intruder had used that to strike Dubois."

Alister continued, "A lot of the furniture was overturned and the contents of a bureau was strewn on the floor. Richard telephoned into the department and asked for a forensics team to be sent to the address. In the meantime I asked Dubois to examine the bureau's contents on the floor and try to determine what if anything had been taken. He busied himself with looking through the items on the floor and mentioned at three different points that his cell phone was gone, his new wristwatch was gone, and his green emerald ring was gone."

Richard put in, "Dubois said that he had owned the ring for years but that he had recently bought the wrist watch and cell phone."

Alister said, "I asked Dubois if he wore his watch and ring regularly. He said he usually didn't wear his ring. He said he had recently bought a new operating system for his old computer. He had installed the new operating system on his old computer, but was having trouble running his old computer and was asking his friends for help. Apparently, he would get stuck out on the Internet."

"I asked DuBois if he mentioned his new watch or emerald ring to his friends," said Alister. "He answered that he sometimes mentioned them while talking to his friends about his computer problem."

Alister continued, "I asked Dubois who he had recently spoken to about the computer. He gave us the names of several people who live in the same building that he lives in. He also gave us the names of several people he is acquainted with at Arnold's Broiler that he spoke to about his computer problem."

Richard said, "The computer wasn't worth much. The watch and ring would be worth a lot more than the computer."

Jefferson asked, "How did you settle on your suspect?"

"We heard about him while questioning the people Dubois spoke to about his computer," answered Alister. "We interviewed all the people Dubois spoke to in his apartment building and all the people he spoke to at Arnold's Broiler. Mr. Siegfried Stone, our suspect, went over to where Dubois was sitting in Arnold's Broiler and listened to him talking to his friends."

Richard said, "So, we went over to where Siegfried Stone lives and interviewed him just like the others. One of the things Stone told us was that he had visited Caspar DuBois a few days before the crime. He said that DuBois and he had coffee during the visit. Stone said that he had dropped his coffee cup and broken it. While picking up the broken pieces Stone said he cut his finger. This left some blood drops on Dubois' rug."

Alister continued, "Siegfried Stone had a swollen and bruised mouth and chin. We knew that Dubois had struck his assailant during the fight. We went back to Arnold's Broiler and asked the bartender and waitresses about Siegfried Stone. They told us that Siegfried Stone had an acquaintance, Mr. Atinsky, who regularly goes down to the swap meets in California to sell merchandise he acquires in Seattle."

"So, we questioned Mr. Atinsky," said Alister, "and found out that he had recently acquired a watch and ring from Siegfried Stone. Atinsky gave us the names and addresses of the two people to whom he had sold those items in California."

Richard said, "I recently went down to California and using Atinsky's records found the two people who bought the watch and ring."

"Do you have the watch and ring?" asked Jefferson.

"Yes, we have both," answered Alister. "We expropriated the watch from Mr. Clarence Bourdeau of Fresno, California using an M-108 form. And, we expropriated the emerald ring from Mr. Orville Svensen of Fresno, California using an M-108 form. Both men purchased their items at the swap meet just east of Fresno a few weeks ago."

Richard said, "This was the swap meet that Edward Atinsky went down to with the watch and ring. Fortunately for us, Atinsky keeps complete records including sales receipts of things sold. He gave us the names and addresses of the people he sold the watch and ring to."

Alister said, "The watch has a serial number inside that you can read if you take the back off the watch. The serial on the watch matches the serial number on the sales receipt that Caspar DuBois had from Emerald City Diamond where he bought the watch."

Richard said, "Unfortunately the emerald ring does not have a serial number. However, Caspar DuBois scratched his initials, CMD, on the inside of the ring band when he acquired the ring from relatives eight years ago. And, they are still on the ring band of the ring we picked up from Orville Svensen."

Alister said, "Richard and I went to the REI sports store on Denny Street to inquire if they had sold a hiking parka to anyone recently. One sales girl was fairly sure that she recognized Stone in a set of photographs I showed her as the man she had sold a parka to recently."

Richard said, "All this information about the computer, watch, and ring might convince a jury. They might wonder a little bit about the testimony of a man who sells merchandise in swap meets in California. And the REI sales clerk wasn't absolutely certain that the man who bought the parka was the person in the police photographs of Stone that we showed her. A skilled defense attorney would merely point out that Stone could have found the watch and ring along the sidewalk when he was out walking one night."

After a pause, Alister continued, "But we do have one very strong piece of evidence from the forensics team assigned to the case."

"Your case isn't very strong at this point, gentlemen," said the prosecutor. "Stone's blood drops in Dubois' apartment could be explained by his cutting his finger there the day before."

"We do have one very strong piece of evidence, however," said Richard.

"What is that?" asked the prosecutor.

Alister leaned forward while presenting their strong point. He said, "Our suspect wore gloves during the robbery. He got a cut on his mouth or cheek where Dubois hit him. When he went down the fire escape to depart the crime scene, he caught or scraped his gloved hand on a jagged bracket that holds the fire escape to the building. The jagged bracket ripped his glove and our suspect left a bloody fingerprint on the metal bracket. Our forensics department and the DNA and fingerprint lab of the FBI in Washington identified it as Stone's fingerprint and his DNA. They got his DNA from a sample of Stone's blood that we sent to them in Washington. The FBI already had Stone's fingerprints and DNA from a previous arrest."

Prosecutor Mark Jefferson struck his desk with his fist and said, "That is strong evidence, gentlemen."

Mark Jefferson then said, "I have scheduled a grand jury meeting this afternoon at 2:00 PM for two other cases. I'll add this case to the list. Let's see," he said, looking through the packet of papers Alister had given him at the start, "have you placed in these papers the FBI report about the bloody fingerprints found on the fire escape?"

"Yes, sir, it is in there," said Alister.

"How about the Pine Street Clinic's report on the injuries of Caspar DuBois?" asked Mark Jefferson.

"Yes, sir, that's in there also," said Alister.

"OK," said the prosecutor. "I will use these two pieces of evidence plus maybe some more to convince the grand jury that there is probable cause to think that a crime was committed. If the grand jury thinks there is probable cause, they will issue an indictment. At that point I will take the case to court and the defendant will be arraigned. An arraignment is a hearing before a judge where the defendant can plea bargain or move to a jury trial."

"The grand jury proceeding should be over about 4:00 PM today," said the prosecutor.

"We will determine where Siegfried Stone is this afternoon," responded Alister.

"If the indictment comes down this afternoon, you can arrest him today," said the prosecuting attorney.

"What about incarceration?" asked Richard. "Should we put him in jail?"

"I don't think so," answered the prosecutor. "He is not likely to flee and he is not a danger to society."

"When do you think he will be arraigned?" asked Alister.

"Today is Friday," said the prosecutor. "He will be arraigned Tuesday in Municipal Court."

Mark Jefferson closed the folder on his desk and looked over at his assistant prosecuting attorney. He said, "If the vote to indict comes down this afternoon from the grand jury, then Alfreda Jones will handle the case for the prosecutor's office."

Alfreda said, "All right, Mark, I'll study the folder you have and consult with the detectives during the next few days."

Alister stepped forward and handed his card to Alfreda Jones. He said, "We will do everything we can to assist you, prosecutor."

With that, Mark Jefferson stood up, indicating that the meeting was over. The stenographer completed her work on the computer and stood up. Alister and Richard left the room. Alister and Richard proceeded down the hallway on their way out of the court house.

CHAPTER 21

"I suppose we should go back to the office and update our records and inform the lieutenant of the progress of the case," said Richard.

"Yeah, our meeting went pretty smoothly," said Alister.

"Do you think that the grand jury will vote to indict?" asked Richard.

"They almost always do. They only hear the prosecutor's side of the story," said Alister.

"Where do you think we will find Siegfried Stone this afternoon?" asked Richard.

"He might be home," answered Alister, "or may be over at Arnold's Broiler having a beer."

They proceeded to the police station and Alister put his briefcase on his desk.

"I see the lieutenant is in his office alone at this minute," said Alister. "Let's go over to his office and acquaint with the progress of the case."

They spent about five minutes in the lieutenant's office telling him what happened at the prosecutor's office. Then they returned to their cubicle and got out their computer to type in the latest information and bring the case up to date.

After about an hour, Alister said, "Let's get lunch

downstairs and then head out and see if we can find Siegfried Stone."

"All right," responded Richard.

The special in the cafeteria was spaghetti with tomato sauce and hot Italian sausage. They both chose that.

When they got to the table and started eating, Richard said, "Suppose we don't find Siegfried Stone at Arnold's Broiler or at home. Where do we look then?"

Alister thought about it a minute and said, "We will have to ask the bartender at Arnold's Broiler and anyone else down there who knows him fairly well where his haunts typically are."

Richard said, "We could also ask Caspar DuBois. They used to be fairly well acquainted."

After lunch they got an unmarked detective car from the garage and drove to Siegfried Stone's apartment.

Richard said, "We don't want to knock on his door or prowl around too much. If we do that, Stone might sense something is up and decide to flee."

"Right," said Alister. "We will just see if his car is there."

When they arrived at 1608 First Avenue, where Siegfried lived, they drove around the building and parked in the alley. They walked to the parking lot that the building used and noticed that Stone's car was missing.

"Let's try Arnold's Broiler," said Richard.

"OK," answered Alister.

They drove over to Arnold's Broiler and went in. The downtown crowd that patronizes Arnold's Broiler when work is over was already showing up. They went over to the lunch counter and sat down. They had their backs to the crowd and so were not likely to be recognized.

The waitress came over and said, "Good afternoon gentlemen. Our special this afternoon is a lovely cheese omelet."

Richard said, "I'll just take a bowl of chili and a coffee, please."

Alister said, "Make mine just coffee, please."

When she left, Richard said, "I'll go to the men's room. I can check the bar on the way and see if Stone's there."

"OK," said Alister.

Richard got up and left. About ten minutes later he returned. "He is in the bar with Edward Atinsky. They are probably talking about Atinsky's next trip to California."

"OK," said Alister.

Alister looked at his watch. "3:30 PM," he said. "I suppose we will hear from the prosecutor's office soon." He paused a minute, and said, "We can go back to the office after you finish your chili. The indictment will probably be in from the court soon."

"Yeah," answered Richard. "Stone will probably stay here for a while longer."

When they got back to the office, they noticed that nothing had come in from the court yet. They sat in their cubicle and waited.

"I wonder how much of our report Mark Jefferson used when speaking to the grand jury," said Richard.

"Well, he had several hours after we left before he met with them," said Alister. "So, I suppose he had time to read a fair amount of it."

"Yes," answered Richard. "And, he knows the people on the grand jury and how they think."

"I heard that the grand jury only hears the prosecutor's

side of things," said Alister. "That seems a bit slanted in the prosecutor's favor. But the defense hasn't even formed up yet."

"Well, the grand jury pretty much decides probable cause and nothing more, I guess," said Richard.

"Probable cause is enough to indict," said Alister. "That's all we need."

"Well, probable cause is enough to arrest," said Richard. "Proving someone is guilty is a thousand times more difficult."

At that moment the lieutenant walked up to their cubicle. "The indictment is in from the grand jury," he said, handing them a paper form. "So, you can go and arrest Siegfried Stone."

Alister and Richard rose and took their guns from their desk drawers. As they took the elevator down to the garage, Alister said, "Let's try his apartment first. If he is not there we will go over to Arnold's Broiler."

"OK," said Richard.

This time they chose a marked police cruiser and set out for 1608 First Avenue. When they arrived, they parked in front of the building in the no parking zone.

They went up to the room 205 and knocked on the door. After a minute, the door was opened by Siegfried Stone.

"What's this?" said Stone.

Alister said, "Siegfried Stone, we are here to arrest you for the assault and robbery of Caspar DuBois at his apartment on Thursday, September 15."

Richard stepped forward and read Siegfried Stone his

Miranda Rights. He then said, "Turn around," and put handcuffs on him.

"Just a minute," said Siegfried Stone. "You have the wrong person. Caspar DuBois is my friend. He even told me about the robbery last week. He said his new wrist watch was taken. I didn't take his things. You've got the wrong person. What makes you even think I took them?"

"You left some telltale evidence at his apartment, Mr. Stone," said Richard.

"Evidence?" said Stone. "I visit with Dubois fairly often. You have misinterpreted something. I demand a defense attorney right now."

"That is your right, and you may telephone one from the police station. But we are taking you to the police station now."

Alister and Richard marched Siegfried Stone down the stairs and over to the waiting police car and put him in the back seat. Alister and Richard got in the front and they proceeded to the police station.

When they arrived at the station, they took Stone to the third floor where they had eight holding cells. They first went to an interrogation room. The room had light beige colored walls with a darker brown band around the bottom of the wall about three feet high going around the room. There was a grey metal table in the middle of the room, with four chairs around it. On one wall was a cabinet and stand that held a miscellany of things, including the fingerprint kit.

Some departments had modern fingerprint equipment that took your prints when you placed your hand on a glass plate. The prints were then immediately sent to the FBI fingerprint catalog in Washington.

However, the police station in Seattle used by Alister and Richard use the old fashioned finger print method. There were cards subdivided into five squares or labeled compartments per card. There was also an ink pad that the suspect put his fingers on before pressing them on the card. Also, in the cupboard were a box of tissues and a bottle of cleaning fluid to use after fingerprinting.

In one corner a white cloth like material was glued or fastened to the wall. A camera mounted on a stand with wheels was pushed up against the wall. There was no glass panel in the wall through which a witnesses could peek at the people sitting at the table in an attempt to identify some culprit they had encountered. That was a common technique used in Hollywood movies but it was not installed in this room.

They sat Stone down in a chair at a table in the room. Alister sat in the chair on the opposite side of the table, while Richard removed the hand cuffs from Stone's wrists.

Stone began, "How did you ever decide to accuse me? What made you think that?" "Well, Siegfried Stone, for one thing we found some of your blood around Edward DuBois' room," said Alister.

"My blood?" said Siegfried.

"Yes, your blood, Stone," said Richard. "We found blood spots in Dubois' room that match your DNA."

Stone pause for a moment. Then he said, "But I was over at Dubois' apartment last week and cut my finger on a coffee cup that I accidentally dropped. You are putting the wrong interpretation on things."

"When I spoke to you a few days ago, you had a swollen and cut lip, Mr. Stone," said Alister. "How did that happen?"

"I told you then," said Stone. "I got into a little scuffle with somebody down at the bar in Arnold's Broiler. We threw a few punches. There was nothing to it."

"We have spoken to a Mr. Atinsky who says he knows you well and that you gave him a wristwatch and ring to sell down in California at some swap meet," said Alister.

"I found that watch and ring in the grass along the sidewalk here in town," said Stone. "I gave them to Atinsky to sell in those California swap meets he goes to. I thought I could get some money for them."

"Well, we have recovered the watch and ring from California and DuBois identifies them as his own," said Alister. "Furthermore, we found your finger prints on the ring."

Stone responded with, "If they are Caspar DuBois' property then I might have touched them while visiting DuBois."

Alister and Richard were trying to get Stone to confess and sign a guilt confession. Stone was still relaxed and composed. He wasn't at all distraught or agitated.

Stone said, "I want a lawyer before I talk to you people again."

"OK, Mr. Stone, said Richard. "But we have to fingerprint you first and take your picture."

Richard got up from the table and said, "Over this way please, Mr. Stone."

Richard went to the stand at the side of the room that held the paraphernalia for fingerprinting. He got out two cards and an ink pad. He took hold of Stone's finger, rubbed it on the ink pad, and rolled in on one of the cards. After doing this to all ten fingers, Richard said, "We send these to the FBI in Washington for entry into their fingerprint catalog." Richard gave Stone a paper towel with some antiseptic on it and said, "You can wipe your hands on this."

Richard then walked over to the corner of the room that had the white cloth cover on the wall. "Please stand here Mr. Stone," he said. "We have to take your picture."

Alister moved a camera over in front of Stone, and they took the standard two mug shots: one photograph from the front and one from the side.

Then Alister said, "The prosecuting attorney's office has decided to not put you in jail. You will be set free tonight."

Stone showed visible relief at hearing this.

"However, Mr. Stone, your arraignment in court has been set for 10 AM next Tuesday morning in the Municipal Court at Second and Columbia," said Alister, handing him the document he had received at the police station. "It is in court room 304."

Stone took the document and looked at it.

"Don't miss the date, Stone," said Richard. "A warrant for your arrest will be issued if you do."

"You will be appointed a lawyer at the arraignment, Mr. Stone," said Alister, "if you don't have one of your own."

With that, Siegfried Stone turned and walked out of the room.

"Do you think he will hire a lawyer of his own?" asked Richard.

"I doubt it," answered Alister. "He probably doesn't have much money. That's why he committed the robbery in the first place."

"Did Stone appear very apprehensive or defensive to you?" asked Richard.

"No, not especially," answered Alister. He thought a moment and then added, "He was a little agitated when I said that Edward Atinsky identified him as the person who gave him the watch and ring to sell in California."

"Yeah, that would be a solid identification," said Richard, "since they had known each other for years."

"Yes, it would stand up in court in front of a jury," commented Alister.

"But proving how the watch and ring came into his possession will be difficult," said Richard.

"He wasn't overly concerned about our finding his fingerprint on the ring," said Alister.

"Well, he has visited Caspar DuBois numerous times. So his fingerprint would naturally turn up on Dubois' possessions," said Richard.

"If it weren't for his bloody fingerprint on the fire escape, we would have a hard time getting a conviction in a jury trial," said Alister.

They turned off the light and left the room. They took the elevator to their floor and entered their cubicle. Most of the officers had gone home or were out on errands. The lieutenant was in his office on the telephone.

Alister and Richard sat down at their desks and checked their e-mail. Alister had an email from Denise thanking him for supper the other night and making a remark about reading tests tonight.

Roland Sikes leaned over the wall of their cubicle and said that a couple of new vending machines had been installed in the hallway on the second floor, just outside the men's and women's lavatories. He said, "Now when Randolphs closes on the first floor at 6:00 PM, we will have more choices around here at 9:00 PM if you're stuck here."

"What's new?" asked Richard.

"Well, they added a microwave and a refrigerated vending machine with some selections of sandwiches," answered Roland.

"That should help some," said Richard.

"I'm going home," said Roland, "I've been here all day. I hear that you two just closed a case. Congratulations."

"Yes, we just made the arrest," said Richard.

"Well, I'm off," said Roland. "See you tomorrow." He walked to the elevators and left.

"I think I'll go home, too," said Alister. "I'll come in tomorrow morning and finish updating my records and filing them."

"Sounds good to me," said Richard. "I'll do the same." They put on their jackets and headed for the elevator.

CHAPTER 22

When Alister got home he left his shoes at the door and went over to the patio door. He opened the blinds and then he opened the glass door. He stepped out and took a deep breath of fresh air. He next went to the refrigerator to see what snacks if any he had. He noticed that he was getting a little low on almost everything. He took out his jar of grape juice and poured himself a cup. He closed the refrigerator and opened the cupboard to peer at his supply of cereals and biscuits. He noticed the ginger snaps with pleasure, and took them out.

OK, he had the cup of grape juice and the box of ginger snaps. He opened the refrigerator and took out a can of beer.

He felt adequately supplied with snacks and headed for the patio. He stepped out on the patio and set the beer and grape juice on the table after taking a sip of grape juice. He opened the ginger snaps, selected one, and started munching.

He looked around at the panorama before him. The weather was still pleasant, 74° and no rain. There had been no rain or overcast for several days now, and Alister was taking in the stunningly beautiful scenery. He could look both south and west from his balcony. He was on the second floor and had an unobstructed view it either direction.

To the west he could see a ferry plying its way across the Sound to Bremerton. The magnificent Olympic Mountains formed the backdrop to the ferryboat scene.

Alister took another couple of ginger snaps and a sip of grape juice and turned his attention to the south. There stood Mount Rainier in its majesty. Alister always marveled at how you always knew Mount Rainier was there, but you couldn't see it through the overcast and cloud cover. And then one day the sky clears up, and you are actually startled by this majestic mountain that is so gigantic and close. Alister could see the snowcap on the mountain that he figured never disappeared.

Alister polished off another ginger snap and then drank the rest of the grape juice. He picked up the can of beer and snapped opened the cover. He began to think about the case.

He began thinking about his long standing theory on solving cases. The detective has a very hard time actually proving anything. He can easily convince himself and almost anyone around him that he has found the real culprit. But proving it is another thing entirely.

Fingerprints and DNA from blood drops help a lot. They take the arm waving gestures out of the case. But the question always remains: who left the fingerprints and blood drops with their DNA and when was it done. Before the crime, at the time of the crime, or after the crime.

Fingerprints and DNA are very, very reliable. But, when were they deposited at the crime scene? Alister knew that DNA can be weakened or destroyed by careless handling by the police officers. But the police are carefully trained in these matters now.

In the present case of Siegfried Stone, for instance, things are not absolutely certain. Alister recalled that Caspar DuBois admitted that Siegfried Stone had been over for a visit a day or so before the robbery and had cut his finger. His bleeding finger left blood drops with their DNA in the apartment. One could say that Siegfried Stone purposely cut his finger to provide an explanation for his DNA appearing in the apartment if a scuffle should develop during his subsequent robbery and he be injured. But that could be regarded as an explanation contrived by the detective inspecting the scene. It is also possible that Siegfried Stone did accidentally cut his finger and that he didn't commit the robbery.

But if someone else committed the robbery, how did Stone's fingerprints get on the fire escape ladder with both Stone's blood and Dubois' blood embedded in the fingerprints?

Alister was pretty sure that he had a pretty good case. He thought that a jury would buy it.

Alister left the balcony and went back inside the living room, closing the balcony door behind him. He decided to read a couple of chapters in the Elmore Leonard novel he was reading.

After about an hour Alister decided to make supper. He put down the novel and went into the kitchen. He opened the refrigerator and scanned its contents. He opened the cupboard door and checked its contents. He realized that he had two choices. He could make spaghetti and meat balls or grilled chicken with rice and vegetables. He chose the chicken dinner and set to work preparing it.

On Monday Alister and Richard arrived at their cubicle early. They knew that they had to review everything and be ready in case the judge at the arraignment called them to testify.

Alister said, "Maybe we should have Ralph Lee from the forensics department here to go over the data."

"He might be called to testify by the judge at the arraignment, that's true," said Richard.

Alister telephoned the forensics department and asked Ralph Lee to attend their meeting.

Ralph Lee arrived several minutes later. "Getting ready for the arraignment, are you? Well nothing much usually goes wrong there," he said.

They spent the rest of the morning reviewing the material and updating records. They then went to lunch at Shorey's on Fifth Avenue.

On Tuesday morning at 10:00 AM Alister, Richard, and Ralph Lee were sitting in court room 304 of the Municipal Court House at Second Avenue and Columbia. Siegfried Stone was ushered in by the court bailiff to a chair at the defense table. He had managed to show up for his arraignment.

At three minutes after 10:00 AM, the bailiff rose and said, "All rise.

Hear ye, hear ye, hear ye.

The Municipal Court of Seattle, USA is now in session.

The honorable Judge Patrick O'Toole presiding.

May God save this honorable court. Be seated, please."

At this point, Judge Patrick O'Toole entered, attired in

a black robe, and seated himself at the bench on the raised dais at the front of the room. He nodded to the clerk of court to proceed.

The clerk of court rose and read from the docket, "This is the arraignment of Mr. Siegfried Stone before the Municipal Court of Seattle.

The judge asked the prosecutor if she was ready. She answered yes, and was told to proceed.

Prosecuting attorney Alfreda Jones rose and addressed the court, "The Municipal Court charges Mr. Siegfried Stone with the assault and robbery of Caspar DuBois in his home on September 15."

The judge looked at Siegfried Stone and asked, "Mr. Stone what is your preference for an attorney? Do you have an attorney of your own, or do you want a court appointed attorney, or do you wish to conduct your own defense?"

Siegfried Stone answered, "I request a court appointed attorney, your honor."

Judge O'Toole looked at some papers on his desk and asked, "Is attorney George Manford in the court?"

An attorney stood up on the left side of the room and answered, "I am attorney George Manford, your honor."

Judge O'Toole said, "Mr. Stone, I appoint Mr. George Manford as your attorney."

At this point George Manford rose and walked over to the defense table and sat down next to Siegfried Stone.

After a few minutes, Judge O'Toole spoke again, "Mr. Siegfried Stone, how do you plead to the charge against you, guilty or not guilty?"

Attorney George Manford answered, "Not guilty, your honor."

The judge asked the court reporter, "Do we have a free day two months from now?"

The court reporter consulted his computer and answered, "We have a free day on November 15, your honor."

The judge responded, "The trial of Siegfried Stone is scheduled for 9:00 AM November 15. The defendant will not be imprisoned and no bail is set."

The judge struck his gavel on the bench and said, "Next case."

The bailiff went up to Siegfried Stone an escorted him and his attorney out of the court room.

Alister and Richard and Ralph Lee also rose and left the courtroom. They met the prosecuting attorney, Alfreda Jones, in the hallway.

Alfreda Jones said, "Let's meet in my office tomorrow morning at 9:00 AM. We have got to get started on the prosecutor's case."

The next morning at 9:00 AM Alfreda Jones, Alister, Richard, and Ralph Lee were seated in one of the conference rooms on the fourth floor of the Municipal courthouse.

Alfreda began, "Good morning gentlemen. It is nice to see you this morning. I have asked John Williamson of the prosecutor's office to attend our meetings and bring his recording equipment. We will probably have to meet several times before the trial and it greatly facilitates matters to have all of our discussions and data on a computer file that has an efficient cataloging and indexing mechanism."

"Alister, please give us an outline of the case that the police department has put together. I am especially interested in the strong evidence that we have. We have to consider how the defense attorney will attempt to weaken or question the evidence."

Alister began, "I realize that robberies don't always lead to jury trials; sometimes there is only a judge presiding. However, in this case there is an assault charge accompanying the theft charge."

Alfreda commented, "The accused, Mr. Siegfried Stone, has requested the trial. He apparently thinks he can win. A defendant has a right to a trial by jury in this country."

Alister said, "I will present our case and especially our evidence. Caspar DuBois was attacked in his apartment on September 15 at approximately 1:00 AM. He was awakened by the sound of someone moving in his bedroom. A struggle commenced and Caspar DuBois was struck on the jaw by a hard object. We are quite sure it was a marble bookend. We have it in evidence and we have found Caspar DuBois' blood and hair on it. The assailant then left the apartment in the same way he entered. He went down the fire escape which is just outside Caspar DuBois' window."

"Caspar DuBois went immediately to a 24 hour health clinic on Fourth Avenue and Pine. We have evidence from that clinic. Siegfried Stone's blood and fingerprints were found on DuBois' bandage. However, Stone was an acquaintance of DuBois and visited his apartment in the past and on one recent occasion cut his finger in DuBois' apartment. Dubois then telephoned the police. Richard Hopkins and I took the call."

"Dubois says he didn't see his assailant clearly because he was wearing a black hiking parka and ski mask. Dubois examined his apartment after we got there and determined that his assailant had taken his new wrist watch and a silver ring with a green emerald inset, that he had owned for years."

"Richard and I canvased several pawn shops in town but found nothing. We interviewed several witnesses at Dubois' apartment and Arnold's Broiler. We found out that Edward Atinsky and Siegfried Stone have business transactions from time to time. Atinsky takes secondhand merchandise to California swap meets and sells it there."

"After conferring with Atinsky, Richard Hopkins made a trip to California and retrieved Dubois' watch and ring. Atinsky maintains accurate names and addresses of the people he sells merchandize to at these California swap meets. We have the serial number of the watch and Dubois identified his ring from an engraving on it. Both the watch and ring have Siegfried Stone's fingerprints on them."

"Now, as to the quality or strength of our evidence. We can prove that the fingerprints on Dubois' watch and ring are Stone's. However, Stone was an acquaintance of Dubois and visited him at his apartment. So, he can say in court that he left his fingerprints on the watch and ring while visiting Caspar DuBois."

"Now, for our strongest piece of evidence. Our forensic team, that conducted an investigation of Dubois' residence after the crime, found a bloody fingerprint on an outdoor metal bracket that attaches the fire escape to the building. We have an FBI report matching fingerprints and blood from the fire escape bracket with those of Siegfried Stone."

Alfreda said, "That does sound solid. I will use your account that you just presented with the written report that you have submitted to construct my case. No doubt, I will have to consult with you people several more times before the trial, but I have enough to get started."

With that the meeting broke up and Alister, Richard, and Albert Lee returned to the police station.

Printed in the United States
By Bookmasters